JOHNNIE D.

A TOM DOHERTY ASSOCIATES BOOK

NEW YORK

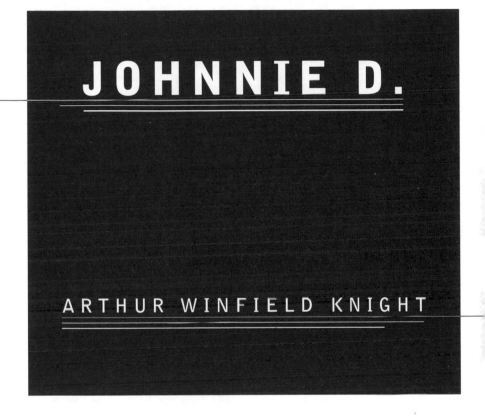

JOHNNIE D.

ARTHUR WINFIELD KNIGHT

This is a work of fiction. All the characters and events portrayed in this novel are either fictitious or are used fictitiously.

JOHNNIE D.

Book design by Victoria Kuskowski

A Forge Book
Published by Tom Doherty Associates, LLC.
175 Fifth Avenue
New York, NY 10010

Forge ® is a registered trademark of Tom Doherty Associates, LLC.

ISBN 0-312-86759-X

First Edition: March 2000

Printed in the United States of America

0   9   8   7   6   5   4   3   2   1

FOR KIT — ALWAYS

"Facts are unforgiving, so fuck facts, make the scenes work."

—JOHN GREGORY DUNNE,
Playland

Thanks to Nat Sobel and Robert Gleason for helping to make this book a reality.

SUMMER 1933

I walk into the bank slowly. There's no hurry.

Hank's behind me, and our driver's in the Chevy out front; I can hear the engine idling until the door to the bank whooshes shut, than all I can hear is the sound my oxfords make as I cross the marble floor. My footsteps echo in the big room.

I smile at the woman in the teller's cage as I approach. It's the noon hour, so she's the only one here. It's a good way to start a new week.

The teller's in her early twenties and her pupils are dilated, as if she put drops of belladonna in her eyes, but it's probably the dim light. I imagine her going home with a headache each night, taking two aspirin with a glass of tepid water, from counting money all day. I'll relieve her of that responsibility.

I pull my .38 out of my coat pocket, aiming it at her. I say, "This is a stickup, honey," trying to sound friendly, as if I were someone asking her out for a date, then I vault over the railing that separates us. I've wanted to do something like that since I saw my first Douglas Fairbanks movie.

It never hurts to be friendly, so I ask the teller her name.

She says, "Margaret. Good," as if her last name were an afterthought.

"That's a good name, Margaret." I smile at her. "Just tell me where the money is, then face the wall and put your hands up. We don't want you to get hurt."

She points toward the vault, breathing hard. "Over there," she says. Her face is pale blue.

I love small towns. The people in them are so trusting.

The vault's open, and I fill the canvas sack I had under

my coat with bills and a collection of old coins. Jesse James couldn't have handled things more smoothly.

There's even a diamond ring in the vault. Margaret says, "It belongs to the daughter of the bank president. She put it there for safekeeping when she went to play tennis." Her voice is muffled because she's facing the wall, along with two customers who came into the bank while I was conducting this transaction. They all have their hands up.

"There's a poetic justice to all this," I say. "Don't you think so, Margaret?" but she doesn't answer.

Hank lines a third customer up against the wall, but the guy's tall so Hank tells him, "Put your damn hands down. People'll be able to see them from the street."

When the sack's full, I signal Hank, and he marches everyone into the vault.

"It's been an honor and a privilege," I say, tipping my straw hat. I shut the vault door.

The president can let them out when he comes back from his lunch at the Elks. People are starving while he stuffs himself and his daughter plays tennis. I've seen the faces of the dispossessed on every street corner in every city I've been to; they're holding signs saying they'll work for food.

Not me.

I worked in a veneer mill and a machine shop, and it was a sucker's game. I did all the sweating while the bosses got richer.

Hank and I get into the backseat of the Chevy, and our getaway man pulls the car out from the curb. He used to be a dirt-track auto racer, and he rounds a corner at eighty as we leave town, the tires squealing, the dust from the country road rising behind us, whirling like a tornado.

I pull some hundred-dollar bills our of the sack, holding them up. "I never did understand why people call it blue Monday," I say.

MARGARET GOOD

I tell the police chief, "He was a nice-looking man. He wore a conservative gray suit and a straw hat, angled so that it would keep the sun out of his eyes. He could have been the nephew of the bank president. I didn't know anything was wrong until he pulled the pistol and told me it was a stickup."

"Then he vaulted over the railing?"

"Yes."

"Why do you think he did that?"

"How should I know?"

"Most people would have walked around the railing."

"Yes, I suppose they would."

"So why didn't he?"

"Maybe he wanted to show off. To let me know how athletic he was."

The chief writes my answers in a small spiral notebook he took from his shirt pocket. He's left-handed. "Why would he want to do that?"

I heard left-handed people are brain-damaged. "Maybe he thought I'd be frightened, that I'd cooperate more readily."

"Did you?"

"What?"

"Cooperate?"

"Yes, of course."

"Besides wearing a gray suit, what did he look like?"

"He was thirty, thirty-one, average height. He had brown hair, and his eyes were gray. He had the biggest-looking gun I ever saw, and it was pointed at me."

"What did the other people do? The ones who came into the bank?"

"Mr. Mowrey seemed angry. He said, 'If I'd had a thimbleful of brains, I'd have known something was going on. I never would have come in here. But by the time I'd figured it out, this guy put a gun in my belly.' He said that while he was standing next to me, and we had our hands up."

"How much money do you think they got?" the chief asks.

"Mr. Bernard told me they got away with thirty-five hundred dollars, and an engagement ring that belonged to his daughter."

"Do you have any reason to doubt him?"

"No. No, of course not."

"Is there anything else?"

"Just one thing. I think the man who vaulted over the railing knew I was a kid and he was sorry to scare me. He didn't want to scare me any worse than he had to."

"What makes you say that?"

"It's just a feeling. I sensed he was a good man."

"Sure, that's why he holds up banks," the chief says.

FRANK MORGAN

I tell the reporter fellow, "He snuck up on me in the night."

There's a gap between his front teeth, and I imagine he whistles when he sleeps.

"It was close to eleven and I'd been workin' all day at the grocery. Some people might think it's an easy life, just standin' there, gabbin' with customers, ringin' up sales, but I work like a nigger.

"It was a Saturday, early September, so it was still hot. My shirt was soaked and I knowed my wife was gonna ask me how come I sweat so much, but she didn't spend all day in no store. I could feel the wood floors buckle from the heat, and my legs hurt, the way they do when you spend all day standin' on them. It was so hot a can of peaches exploded."

The reporter fellow nods, writin' it all down in a spiral notebook he took from his shirt pocket. It looks like he's usin' some type of code, but he says it's called shorthand.

"I was passin' this alley, Broad Alley it was, next to the Mooresville Christian Church when someone leaps out at me. He had a heavy bolt wrapped in a handkerchief, and he hit me on the head, then he pulled a pistol but I grabbed hold of it.

"We stood there swayin' back and forth like we was doin' some kind of weird dance, and I could tell he'd been drinkin' moonshine. It was on his breath.

"Then the gun went off and I started yellin', 'Bloody Jesus! Help, help!' Some friends from the Pollock Club across the street come runnin', and the punk who'd hit me took off down the street.

"I don't think anyone would have knowed it was John Dillinger, but he run by two teenaged girls who was sittin' on the steps of the Keller home opposite the Mooresville High School and they recognized him.

"Some bleedin' hearts thought Johnnie ought to go free because it was his first offense and he'd always been a good boy, but I had to have eleven stitches where he hit me with that bolt, and I wasn't forgettin' it. Them bleedin' hearts could say all they wanted about Johnnie bein' a kid, but he was twenty and married and he'd been in the navy 'till he went AWOL. Johnnie ought to have knowed better.

"I told Judge Williams he ought to throw the book at Johnnie, but I even thought Johnnie's sentence was too severe when I heard it.

"Williams give him ten to twenty years for conspiracy to commit a felony, and for assault with intent to rob.

"I know Johnnie and his family was bitter about it. Old

John blamed himself because he couldn't afford no lawyer, and he'd told his son he knowed the judge would be lenient if Johnnie just told the truth and pleaded guilty. So much for the truth, I say."

"Do you think justice was served?" the reporter fellow asks.

"Maybe. I don't know. Judge Williams sent a young man away that day, but a criminal come back in his place eight and a half years later. I know that much."

JOHN DILLINGER

Singleton's standing next to the Coke cooler at the gas station when I pull up to the pumps. The fingers on his left hand are webbed, and he's holding a bottle. He probably wonders if I came looking for him.

He ought to wonder.

I get out of the car and tell the attendant, "Fill 'er with ethyl," and I remember a girl named Ethel. She hated it when people said you could go farther with ethyl.

I'll always remember Singleton.

"It's been a long time, Ed."

"Yeah. How are you, John?"

"I could be better."

"Yeah, I imagine."

Singleton's face is ruddy in the red light. But everyone looks ruddy to me since I got out of stir. All the guys I know are pale from being locked up. They only let us into the yard to play baseball. We were lucky if we saw the sun once a week.

Singleton swats at a mosquito, crushing it against his cheek with his right hand, still holding the Coke bottle in his left.

"What kind of a car are you driving these days?"

"What kind of a question is that?" Ed asks, but he points

to a Ford parked beside the rest rooms. Maybe he's waiting for somebody to come out. Maybe he's become a can hanger.

He was sitting behind the wheel of a Ford the last time I saw him, and it was summer. He told me, "It'll be easy. Morgan's an old guy. All you have to do is tap him on the head, then grab the money. I hear he goes home with a hundred bucks on a good night. I'll be waiting for you."

He gunned the engine as I walked down the street toward Morgan's store, holding the handkerchief with the bolt, the pistol in my pocket. We'd been drinking all night, lying on the grass next to the library, looking up at the sky. There were two moons.

When I ran down the street where Singleton was supposed to be a few minutes later, he was gone.

The getaway man. Gone.

I knew he drank too much and I got tired of his bragging, but I didn't expect him to skip out on me. He'd already been in prison, and was always talking about it. He said, "You have to let time serve you, Johnnie. Don't serve time." I never knew what he meant.

He had a lousy job at the Mooresville Electric Light Company, and he was an umpire for the games in our league. He was always in a bad mood. My stepmother said he had a wife who nagged him and a bunch of crying kids. I remember I swung my bat at him when he called a low ball a strike and told me I was out. I never should have trusted him.

He told Judge Williams a sad story and got off with two years, even though Ed had planned the robbery.

"You're sweating, Ed."

There's blood on his cheek where he squashed the mosquito.

"Yeah, it's a hot one."

He takes a soiled handkerchief from his back pocket, wiping his forehead.

I'd like to squash him, I'd like to pay him back for all those nights I ate meat and boiled potatoes. They called it baked hash or Hungarian goulash or Irish stew, but it was always the same.

All you could hear was the men around you chewing and the rattle of the knives and forks on tin plates. You could smell the disinfectant they used when they swabbed the floor and the rancid meat and the body odor of the men around you. Three thousand nights of meat and potatoes. Three thousand days working in the upholstery shop, the fibers coming up into your nose. I still have trouble breathing when I go into a room where the furniture's stuffed.

"You're in luck," I say.

"How's that?"

"I'm not a killer."

I pay the attendant, then I point my index finger at Singleton and smile.

"Bang."

Singleton doesn't smile.

"Bang, bang."

"Don't," he says.

"You've got to develop a sense of humor, Ed."

"It's not funny, Johnnie."

"I look at it this way. Those eight and a half years in the joint gave me a new career."

"What's that?" Singleton asks.

"I rob banks."

MARIE LONGNAKER

Johnnie lies on his back, naked, beneath the ceiling fan. The blades go *whack, whack, whack,* like somebody slapping the wall with a wet towel. It gets on my nerves, but nothing bothers Johnnie after he's made love. His body glistens in the heat. The fan just moves the hot air around.

After we made love the first time he said, "I get terrible headaches if I don't do it at least once a day."

"You won't get any headaches while I'm around," I said.

We've opened the windows on both sides of our room, but there's no wind and I wonder why they call Chicago the Windy City.

Johnnie gets up, his phallus still partially erect. It seems huge, dangling before him like some kind of divining rod. He could be dowsing for water.

"Johnnie, you're divine," I say and he looks pleased.

He touches his .45, as if he needs to feel it to know it's there. He set it on the bureau next to our bed before we made love. It gave me an odd feeling the first time he did that; I kept staring at the pistol. It was gleaming, metallic, and I wondered if he'd ever killed anyone.

He says, "I have two pistols, one for shooting and one for fun."

"I like the one for fun," I say.

He lights a Lucky Strike and says, "I'm not superstitious, but you need all the luck you can get in my business," then he blows a smoke ring out the window.

We can see Lake Michigan in the distance. Huge clouds are reflected in the water. It's an upside-down world, and the buildings are curiously flat, one-dimensional, in the noon light.

"The air's so still I could balance a feather on your breast," Johnnie says.

"You should have stolen one from Sally Rand's fan," I say. "You were close enough." He threw dollar bills onto the stage at the Colonie Nudiste while she danced.

Johnnie puts his cigarette out in an ashtray with the words, THE HOTEL CRILLON, FOR DISCRIMINATING GUESTS. Then he hands me a small box from the dresser drawer. "I want you to have this."

The box is made out of black velvet, and there's a diamond ring inside. The solitaire sparkles when I put it onto my finger.

"Johnnie. . . ." I don't know what else to say. The stone must be a full karat, set in a platinum band.

"It was my mother's engagement ring," he says. "She died when I was three, so I never knew her. My older sister, Audrey, raised me until my father remarried, then my new 'mom' took over the job." He seems pensive. "She had a stroke while she was baking a cake for my half-brother's birthday and died a couple of hours before I got home from prison. People are always dying on me."

"I won't die on you, Johnnie. Not for a long time," I say, and we hug each other, our bodies slick with sweat, his sex rising.

JOHN DILLINGER

I take a picture of Marie standing in front of the Colonie Nudiste. She sucks her finger and says, "Would you like a lollipop, big boy?" while kids run down the midway and a band goes *oompah* in the distance. Marie's voice is husky, like Jean Harlow's, and her blond hair glistens in the sun.

I wish I could capture it all with my Kodak—the Ferris wheels and the bands and the barkers telling you to step right up and see Schlitzy the Pinhead, the sword swallower, and Jo Jo the Dog-faced boy—but it's too big.

I take another photo of Marie, smiling, so you can see the gap between her teeth, and another of her leaning toward me, her blouse falling away from her breasts so you can see the cleft between them.

Someday she can show the pictures to her kids and say,

"A famous outlaw took them at the World's Fair right after he gave me his mother's engagement ring."

I wish I could photograph my sister making fried chicken, the late afternoon light coming through her kitchen window, flour on her hands and face, the grease sizzling in the cast-iron pan. I wish I could photograph Sally Rand with her pink-and-white fans made of ostrich feathers. I wish I could capture my father leaning against his John Deere tractor, the proudest man in the world, an elbow cocked against one of the huge tires, or the people lining up on the midway to see Henry/Henrietta, the hermaphrodite.

I can hear a barker yelling, "Can you whip a kangaroo, an eighty-pound ape?" over the crack of the .22 rifles from the shooting gallery. Someone else yells, "Everybody's a winner, step right up!"

I can smell hamburgers frying when we pass a large red-and-white tent, and hot dogs are rotating on a spit. I can smell the cotton candy, and I remember eating it until I threw up one summer when I was five and the carnival came to town. I was riding the merry-go-round.

Marie and I approach a cop wearing a white pith helmet and a blue uniform that must have belonged to the Keystone Kops. He's a red-faced Irishman who probably has a name like Dinty Moore, and I know he spends his off-duty hours at a pub disguised as a Chinese laundry. You ask for John Barleycorn when you enter the place. I've probably had a drink with him there. One cop looks like another.

"Officer, would you mind taking our picture? We're newly married."

I hand the camera to the cop, and he holds it at waist level, looking at us through the lens. He could be staring at his feet.

"Smile," the cop says, "When I say *cheese*."

I can smell the lemon rinse in Marie's hair, and I get a hard-on when I put my arm around her. I wonder if it will show in the photo.

"Cheese," the cop says. "That was some grin you had."

I ask, "Would you mind if my wife took a picture of the two of us? I wanted to be a policeman when I was younger, but my asthma kept me off the force."

"That's too bad," the cop says. "It's a great life, it is."

"It's one of my major disappointments. I would have liked the excitement."

"You spend most of your time handin' out parkin' tickets, you do, but there are some excitin' moments."

"Have your ever gone after a famous criminal? Someone like Dillinger?"

"No, but I'd like to get me hands on him, I would. He's a dangerous one."

"Maybe he's not really so bad. Some people even think he's a hero because he robs banks. One fourth of the people in this country can't find a job, and the banks take away their homes."

"Oh, he's a mean one all right. Some of me friends on the force will vouch for that. He's a desperate character. They've shot it out with him on some bloody streets."

They must have seen too many Jimmy Cagney movies. I haven't shot it out with anyone, but he's probably prophetic.

Marie aims the camera and says "cheese," then clicks the shutter. I don't know why people say *cheese* when they want you to smile. It's strange.

People will look at this photo a hundred years from now, and we'll still be the same age. And it will still be the summer of 1933 at the Chicago World's Fair. People will say, "Dillinger had a lot of nerve, having his picture taken with a cop."

Marie and I thank him for posing with me, then the cop and I shake hands.

I say, "Good luck with Dillinger."

"Oh, we'll get him if he shows up here in Chicago, but I think he knows better. He might be able to elude the hicks they have for cops in Indiana, but he won't show his face around here any time soon."

"You don't know how much safer that makes me feel," I say.

SALLY RAND

He's standing in the front row, watching me move the fans. He needs a shave, and he seems to be smiling, even when he isn't.

I put rouge on my nipples and powder on my pudenda, but he won't see anything that intimate. Rand's hands are too quick with the fans. They say that in all the papers.

I saw Pavlova dance when I was six. I knew dancing was going to be part of my life that night, but I didn't know I'd be dancing nude.

I wanted to perform "White Birds Fly in the Moonlight" because I'd watch the white herons swoop down to the pond behind my grandpa's barn, their gosssamer wings outstretched, glistening, when I was a little girl. I imagined what it must be like to glide through the air.

When I began to dance, I tied wings on my shoulders and imagined I was Pavlova performing "The Swan," but my first role on the stage was as Lady Godiva. I've been naked ever since.

I watch the man in the front row, his right hand in front of his pants. He's smiling, moving his hand as if he's trying to keep time with me, making time. Touching himself. He watches me.

When my act's done, he follows me backstage to my dressing room, and I wonder how he got past the doorman.

"You aren't supposed to be here," I say.

"I know."

"It's off-limits."

"A lot of things are these days."

"There are laws against indecent exposure." I sound absurd, saying it. I was arrested four times in one day when I started to perform here. "You're lucky you weren't arrested."

"People tell me that all the time."

When he grins, it's as if he knows something other people don't, but it's more than that. You can tell he likes being alive. It's in the light behind his eyes.

"When I read you make a thousand a week dancing, I had to see your act. Hell, I can't make that much robbing banks," he says, laughing, and I realize I'm talking to the most wanted man in America.

MARIE LONGNAKER

We have lunch at a place called the Burger Barn when we arrive in Michigan City. Johnnie eats two burgers with red onions, dill pickles, and lots of mustard, but he's always hungry.

"I'll miss these if I ever get to Mexico," he says, wiping his chin with a paper napkin.

"I don't know why you never gain weight," I say, and he smiles.

"It must be the active life I lead."

After lunch, I tell him I'd like to visit my brother, Jimmy. I'm in no hurry to get back to Dayton. There's nothing for me there but an apartment that seems too big when Johnnie's gone, and an estranged husband who likes to use his fists on women.

"Maybe I could take Jimmy a basket of fruit or something," I say. "He gets tired of meat and potatoes all the time."

"I know the feeling," Johnnie says, and we stop at a roadside fruit stand near the prison. Johnnie fills a brown-paper sack with bananas, plums, apples, oranges, and grapes. You're supposed to package everything separately and weigh it on the rusting scale next to the produce, but Johnnie never was good at following rules. He gives the clerk a five-dollar bill, and tells him, "Keep the change. I know times are hard."

The clerk's a little bald-headed guy with a face like a horse. I expect him to whinny, but he says "thanks." I'll bet this is the first time he's smiled since the country went dry in 1920. He has a yellow complexion and a bad liver.

Johnnie's wearing a straw hat and the sleeves on his white shirt are rolled up, but he's sweating when he stops the car in front of the prison. He and Jimmy served time together.

"Tell your brother I said hello," Johnnie says, "and give him this."

Johnnie drills a hole into the top of a banana with a penknife, then he rolls up a fifty-dollar bill wrapped in a piece of paper, sliding it into the banana. He stops up the hole with banana pulp, tapping it with his finger.

"Thanks, Johnnie."

I kiss him on the cheek, then get out of the car. The engine's idling.

Some convicts are working in a field down the road while a guard on a horse watches them, holding a rifle. I wonder what kind of a man would have a job like that.

Before I get to the prison, I turn around, blowing Johnnie a kiss.

He waves and yells, "Tell Jimmy to eat the banana first!" Then I walk through the main gate.

JOHN DILLINGER

I park the Essex in front of the sewage-disposal plant, then walk up the dirt path to the pumping station. Pleasant Hill stinks.

An old guy wearing a Yankees baseball cap leans against the door to the office.

"Howdy," he says. His chin looks like it collapsed because he doesn't have any teeth.

"Is Howard Longnaker around?"

"Yeah."

"I'd like to talk with him."

"Well, you don't need no appointment to talk with Howard."

The old guy tries to laugh, but it sounds like he's spitting. He yells, "Hey, Howard, there's someone here to see you."

Howard's eyes are bloodshot, and he blinks when he comes out of the office. He has hairy ears.

"I hear you like to beat up on women."

"What's it to you?" he asks.

His striped overalls are grimy, and there's dirt under his fingernails. He looks like he's spent his life cleaning out crappers and septic tanks. I wonder how Marie stood it when he touched her. He probably smelled of sewage, even after he took a shower.

"You look shitty," I say. "It must be part of your job description."

"Who the hell do you think you are, comin' here and insultin' me?"

"I'm a friend of Marie's," I say.

"Big fuckin' deal."

"I don't want no trouble around here," the old guy says. He looks around, squinting in the sunlight, tugging at the brim of his baseball cap. "I don't want no trouble."

I tell Howard, "Maybe you'd like to take a swing at me, or don't you punch men?"

"I don't have to explain myself to you."

"Marie wants to know where the kids are."

"It's none of her goddamned business."

"You can tell me then."

"Go take a flyin' fuck at a rollin' doughnut," Howard says, then my fist connects with his nose and it sounds like someone snapping the wishbone on a turkey.

The old guy shouts, "Orth, hey Orth, come here quick!"

Howard's nose is bleeding, and he's backed against the wall of the office. I'm holding him up with jabs to his stomach. I keep hitting him, thinking of what he did to Marie, and the blows have a nice rhythm to them. Right, left, right, left.

I came to her apartment moments after he beat her the last time. She stood there in the dim light that came through the shades, crying. She didn't want me to see the bruises on her breasts. They were like shadows across the moon.

I said, "You'll be all right, I promise, but the guy who did this to you won't."

Howard's face is puke-colored, and the broken nose makes him look cross-eyed. He has to breathe through his mouth. You could stuff an apple into it if he opened it any further, and he gasps when I hit him again.

The old guy is pulling at my shirt while someone else chokes me from behind. Orth says, "Stop it. For Christ sake, you're killin' him."

That's a nice thought, but I'm not.

When I stop hitting Howard, he slumps to the ground, lying there with his face in the dirt. He looks good that way.

Orth pulls a .45 from a shoulder holster and says, "You're under arrest. I'm a constable, and I'm takin' you in for assault."

"Sure, fine," I say. He's not taking me anywhere.

What kind of a name is "Orth"? Maybe it's short for something, but I can't imagine what. His parents must have hated him. I'll bet he was an ugly little kid.

The old guy's trying to help Howard get up as I start the car. Orth stands on the running board, pointing the .45 at me. He has a face like an orangutan.

"That way," Orth says, gesturing toward Pleasant Hill with his pistol.

I'm doing fifty by the time I hit the main highway. The tulip trees are flowering, and the colors blur as we pass them. I'm doing sixty, seventy.

Orth holsters his gun and says, "Slow down."

He's hanging onto the car door with both hands as we go by a cornfield. Some Burma Shave signs are nailed to the fence posts, but I'm going too fast to read them, the sky rushing past us.

I hit the brakes when we come to a corner, and I can feel the car skidding. I slam the palm of my left hand into Orth's face so he loses his grip, falling backward into the empty air.

"I bet you were an ugly kid!" I yell, then I speed on down the highway past the flowering tulip trees.

MARIE LONGNAKER

I tell Johnnie, "Howard's vicious. He'll sic the cops on you."

"I already dealt with the cops," he says. "The one who tried to arrest me at the sewage plant was so stupid he jumped—backwards—off the running board of a speeding car."

Johnnie laughs and I tell him, "It isn't funny. You shouldn't take so many chances."

"People have been telling me to play it safe all my life, but the safe things are just the things that people have been doing so long they've worn the edges off. I read that when I was in prison and, right away, I knew what the author meant. I knew I was never going to do anything safe again."

Johnnie and I walk along the street, holding hands. We

pass a Chinese laundry and a furniture store with a sign in the window: TRY STONES FOR SOFT BEDS. I wonder how a stone can be soft.

I say, "The trouble with living on the edge is that you can fall off," but Johnnie just shrugs. He believes we all lead dangerous lives, but some are more dangerous than others.

We pass farmers and their wives and kids on the street. A few of them still come into town in wagons pulled by two horses, but most of them have cars now. The horses leave their droppings in the street, and you can tell the kids are embarrassed. Some of them are so poor they don't wear shoes during the summer, and their feet are blistered.

The families come into Dayton every Saturday to buy raffle tickets because the winner gets a cow. Howard used to buy a string of tickets every Saturday.

I kept asking what he'd do with a cow if he won one, and he didn't know. He just liked the idea of winning something, probably because he'd always been a loser. He'd get up every Saturday morning and say, "It's Cow Day," like it was a big deal. I never discouraged him, because it kept his mind off sex.

Johnnie and I sit in a booth at Geezer's Pharmacy and order a chocolate sundae with vanilla ice cream.

Johnnie tells our waitress, "We want extra syrup, lots of whipped cream, and a cherry on top. And two spoons, please. We're sharing."

The waitress looks like she turned sixteen last week. She's wearing a red-and-white striped blouse that makes her look like a candy cane. She smiles when she takes our order, writing it down, as if getting it correct is the most important thing in the world to her. She probably hasn't discovered boys yet.

"I used to bring the kids in here," I say. "Little Howie always ordered a chocolate cone and the ice cream always dribbled onto his chin. His brother was the neat one."

We feed each other spoonfuls of ice cream when our

waitress brings the sundae, and we sit in the sun coming through the window of Geezer's. I wipe some whipped cream off Johnnie's nose with a paper napkin, wishing everyday were Cow Day.

I say, "I wanted a boy and a girl, but it didn't turn out that way."

"I thought I was going to live happily ever after when I married Beryl, but she divorced me while I was in prison." Sometimes Johnnie lives in an empty room behind his eyes, and I don't know how to reach him. "The day I got the news, I assaulted a guard, and they stuck me in the hole for a week after they'd fractured a couple of my ribs with their batons."

I reach out, squeezing Johnnie's hand, and he spoons the cherry into my mouth.

"I saved it for you," he says. "There's something special about a cherry."

"Yeah."

I can still see the sign—TRY STONES FOR SOFT BEDS—in the window down the street, and I remember lying on a bed of stone. It was autumn and the orange-and-lemon–colored leaves covered our bodies as the boy and I lay next to the river. He told me it wouldn't hurt, but he lied.

"If a pregnant woman bares her belly to the moon, she'll have a girl," I say. "I read that after I'd had the boys."

"You read a lot of things," Johnnie says.

"You have to do it over and over for it to work. Probably it's not true, but I wish I'd tried it."

"Here, have some more ice cream," Johnnie says. "You know what they say about wishing."

JOHN DILLINGER

Beryl and I were married by a justice of the peace on a Saturday afternoon in April. The room smelled of stale cigar smoke, and there was a dirty window above the porcelain sink in the corner. I could see the dirt under the J.P.'s fingernails as he held the Bible, and I knew why Beryl had wanted a church wedding.

It was raining when we left the courthouse.

Beryl was wearing a long white dress, white shoes with high heels, and she had a red rose in her hair. She stumbled going down the courthouse steps, getting the hem of her dress wet. She looked at it as I helped her into the car.

She said, "Oh, shit," and I smiled because she hardly ever swore.

I'd read Jesse James was married in April, too, and I wished I'd had a wedding like his. He rode into Kearney, 50 years before, late in the afternoon. He was mounted on his best horse, and he was wearing a canvas duster over his black suit, at least that's how I like to imagine him: with a starched white shirt with ruffles down the front and a silk tie. And I can't forget his gun belt or the Colt in its holster.

He was going to be married by an uncle who was a preacher.

Jesse rode past the hotel, his leg resting against the rifle in its scabbard, nodding to the people who stood on the porch. It had rained earlier that morning, but it was clear now and he could smell the damp earth as he passed a grocery store, his blue eyes blinking.

Jesse passed the blacksmith stable, and the white clapboard house where his stepfather had practiced medicine before the Yanks hung him.

Dr. Samuel didn't die, at least not that afternoon, but the Yanks had shut off the oxygen to his brain as they raised and lowered him on the rope, and he'd never been right after that. He died in a home for the insane in the town where Jesse was murdered.

I was wearing a secondhand suit my stepmom bought me at the Salvation Army store. She said it was almost as good as new, but you could see the cuffs were frayed, and the suit was too tight around my shoulders. The suit was navy blue, and I was wearing brown oxfords.

I didn't know much at twenty, but I knew I lacked style, and I could feel the sweat trickle down my sides as I got into the car.

Two detectives came to the house, looking for Jesse, just before he and Zee were married. She hid between the feather bed and the mattress in the room where her sister slept, while Jesse hid in the barn. Then a friend rode off on a fast horse, headed for Liberty.

When the detectives set off in pursuit, Jesse and Zee were married.

It was a story the family liked to tell.

I wanted my life to be exciting, but there was just the mud on Beryl's dress and the hard rain and her father. He drank too much and was always eating rope licorice, and he didn't like to take baths.

The house smelled of dusty farts, licorice, and beer, and his great white belly hung over his belt. He liked to brag he'd never read a book, and he owned his house, free and clear. When we told him we were married, he slapped me on the back and said, "Har, har, har, boy, she's all yours," and I winced.

It's raining when I drive to the apartment where Beryl and I lived, and I remember it was always raining that spring. I'd go for long walks in the rain because the apartment was small and airless and I had trouble breathing, even when the windows were open. We were on the first floor, and the neighbor above us was an insomniac. I'd lie in bed listening to his footsteps on our ceiling.

Beryl said, "I'm lonely. All I do is wait for you to come home, then you don't talk to me. You say you're too tired, but you're not too tired to go to the pool hall after dinner every night."

She was sure everything would be better if we had a baby. "Then I'd have someone to take care of, someone to talk to," she said. "I'd have a purpose."

"We've got a whole lifetime to have kids. What's the hurry?"

She was sixteen.

"My mother was only seventeen when I was born," Beryl said.

I could hear the rain hitting the tin gutters on the roof of the apartment, and it gave me the jitters.

"Why don't we talk about it later?" I said.

"I don't want to talk about it later," Beryl said. "I want to talk about it now," but I put my coat on and went outside into the hard rain.

I cross the flooded street to the apartment house and go onto the porch. The paint's peeling and I can smell the stale air from the apartment when a young woman comes to the door. She's wearing a beige dress, and her face seems gray in the drab light.

I show her a photo of Beryl taken shortly after we were married. She was supposed to send me a photo of herself in a bathing suit when I was in prison, but she never did. All I got were the papers saying she'd filed for a divorce.

"Do you know this woman?" I ask. I'll tell Beryl I'm sorry if I ever see her again. I wanted to make the marriage work, but I was only twenty and lost. "She lived here about ten years ago, and her name was Beryl Dillinger."

"I've only lived here six months," the woman says. She seems suspicious. "Dillinger? Like the gangster?"

I nod. "Maybe you know where her parents went. They lived in Martinsville too. Their name was Hovius."

"I never heard of them," the woman says. She's wearing

a babushka to cover the curlers in her hair. "Say, what are you, a bill collector or something?"

"Something," I say, then I cross the street to my car, the dirty water swirling around my ankles.

JOHN HERBERT DILLINGER

"Johnnie was always a good boy," I tell the reporter. He come to Mooresville from Indianapolis to talk with me.

I used to run a grocery store in Indianapolis, but there was too many cars there.

The fellow from the paper and I sit on my porch sippin' lemonade. The glass sweats in my hand, and the moon looks like a lemon in the sky. I hear an owl hoot from the barn.

"I'll tell you one thing," I say. "Johnnie didn't do nothin' any other boy wouldn't have done: play hooky, steal cherries out of somebody's orchard. He used to play ball pretty good, too. He and some other kids had a kind of little neighborhood team. Johnnie liked to pitch, and would play the infield.

"When he wasn't playin' baseball he was generally out huntin'. He was handy with a gun and a dead shot. We always had plenty of rabbits, squirrels, and possums during the open season. Johnnie got his love of huntin' from me. There's nothing I'd rather do when I'm not workin' the farm.

"But Johnnie said farmin' gave him the hay fever. Maybe it did. I know he was sneezin', and he said life here was too slow. He was born and raised in Indianapolis, you know, and I guess the city kind of got a hold on him. If we'd moved here sooner, who knows how things would of turned out?"

JOHN DILLINGER

"I don't like the look of it," Hank says when we pull up in front of the bank. He's sitting beside the driver, and Baby Face and I are in back. He's twenty-five, but he looks like he could be the smallest kid in the tenth grade.

"It looks fine to me," Baby Face says. "You've just got the shakes from drinkin' too much."

"Aw, shut up," Hank says, wiping the sweat from his face with a red handkerchief.

"Pretty soon we'll have to call you 'Shakes,'" Baby Face says. He has a Thompson submachine gun cradled on his lap. He calls it his baby, and I've heard him cooing to it while he strokes the barrel. He'll say, "It's like a lullaby when I pull the trigger, a lullaby of death."

"We can't sit here all day," the driver says. "People will wonder what we're doin' after awhile."

"We'll tell them we're seein' the sights," Baby Face says. He has a smile like a demented child. "We're seein' the sights in beautiful downtown Bluffton." The words come out funny because he's chewing gum.

Hank and I go into the bank while Baby Face stands on the marble steps leading to it. He's wearing a raincoat, like someone selling French postcards, so he can hide the Thompson.

Hank goes to the third window, the one farthest from the street, and hands the teller a five-dollar bill.

"I'd like change for this," Hank says. "Three singles, a dollar in nickels and another in dimes."

When Hank gets the change, he pulls his pistol and says, "This is a stickup," and I leap over the railing separating me from the bookkeeper.

"Where're the other employees?" I ask.

"They're at lunch," the bookkeeper says.

"What do you think of that?" Hank asks. "These two sweethearts are left in charge of everything."

The teller's a thin guy with a squeaky voice, and the bookkeeper's beefy. They remind me of Laurel and Hardy.

Hank stuffs the money from the tellers' drawers into a gunnysack while I cover Laurel and Hardy with my .45.

"There has to be more money than this," Hank says, sticking his pistol in Laurel's face. "Where is it?"

Laurel points to a huge safe built into the back wall and says, "It's . . . it's over there, but the safe's on time lock."

"I'm getting to hate technology," Hank says, then a whistle begins to blow in the distance.

"What the hell is that?" I ask.

"It's the whistle from the waterworks," Laurel says.

"It always goes off at noon," Hardy adds.

I tell Hardy, "Now you're supposed to say, 'This is another fine mess you've gotten us into,'" but he doesn't smile. I ought to leave him some change so he can buy a sense of humor.

Several people are crossing the street, coming toward the bank, but I don't know if they're coming because of the whistle or because the car's parked out front or because Baby Face is standing there in his raincoat and there isn't a cloud in the sky. Maybe they come to check on their savings accounts everyday. Maybe they're damn fools.

"We'd better get out of here," Hank says.

I can hear Baby Face yelling, "What do you think this is, a sideshow? Get the fuck outta here," and I wonder if he's swallowed his gum. Then he pulls out his Thompson, firing a burst over their heads.

The waterworks whistle is still blowing and now an alarm begins to sound on the far wall of the bank. I'm glad we left Baby Face outside, or Laurel and Hardy would be dead.

I gesture toward them with my pistol. "Get down. *Now*. Down on the floor."

Baby Face is still firing the Thompson when Hank and I leave the bank, and I watch the windows breaking at the Hardwick Pool Hall, Patterson's Barbershop, and Greding's Hardware Store. Shards of glass sparkle in the sunlight like deadly raindrops.

A woman pushing a baby carriage begins to scream when she's hit with a glass splinter. I can see the blood blossoming from her forehead as Hank and I run toward the car.

"I haven't had this much fun since I kicked a Sister of Mercy in the shins," Baby Face says. He claims he hates authority because he was raised in a convent in Chicago.

Our driver pulls out from the curb before we can slam the doors on the Chevy. They're flapping in the wind as he speeds by a white-brick funeral home with a tattered awning. "Jesus, that was the longest five minutes of my life," he says, gunning the car north on Highway 75.

Baby Face pulls his door shut. "Don't be a pussy. We can get our ashes hauled at this whorehouse I've been to in Toledo. They have matinee rates if you get there before five, and it ain't more than ninety minutes away if you quit yappin'. Drive," he says.

PENNY HANCOCK

"Johnnie was always my favorite uncle," I tell the reporter. He's wearing a felt hat like the one James Cagney had in *Public Enemy*. I saw that movie three times. My girlfriends and I sat in the loges at the Dream Theatre and smoked cigarettes.

"Tell me about your uncle," the reporter says. He's a couple of years older than I am, in his early twenties, and he drives his own Ford. I bet he drinks bootleg whiskey on Saturday nights and picks up girls in Indianapolis. He has a special horn on his car that goes *ooga ooga*. He showed me. I'll bet he has hot hands.

"Before Uncle Johnnie was sent to prison, he and I used

to go to this little grocery store in Maywood and buy chewing gum at a penny a pack. I remember lying flat on the floor, our heads together, trying to see who could chew the most gum. And we used to play catch when I was seven or eight. Johnnie loves baseball."

"What else can you tell me?"

The reporter and I walk down the lane toward the main road. I know the name of every flower and tree along the way: peony, wild rose, violet. Walnut, willow, buckeye. The reporter kicks at the dust, pigeon-toed.

"Johnnie never had a violent temper, no matter what the papers say about him—or that horrible Mr. Hoover. But Johnnie did have definite likes and dislikes. If he didn't like some food, he wouldn't try it."

"How did he know he didn't like a food he wouldn't try?"

"The same way you know there are some people you wouldn't like. You just look at them and you know they're ugly or mean. Johnnie always said he didn't like green things, like artichokes or green olives, because they're ugly, but he loves avocados with lemon juice. He tried to get me to eat them, but the lemon stung my lips."

I look inside the mailbox when we reach the main road. Empty, the box is empty. I slam the metal lid back, and the red flag on the side wavers. Sometimes I think the postman speeds up when he sees me and he doesn't have a letter to deliver.

I stood here for hours, waiting, when Johnnie was in prison.

I tell the reporter, "I wrote to him every week—ten- , twelve- , fifteen-page letters. I told him when I bought my first lipstick and when I went to my first party and had my first date. When I visited him at Michigan City, he used to ask what I intended to do when I got out of school and I told him I wanted to open a beauty salon.

"He kidded me about getting his fingernails fixed and

keeping his hair from thinning. Told me he'd be a good customer and drum up business for me, but he never discussed what he wanted to do when he got out. I don't think he ever had any intention of living the kind of life he does now.

"If only one person had cared enough to say, 'I'll take him into business with me,' or had given him a chance—given him a feeling he could be useful, I really believe everything would have turned out differently."

"Isn't that a pretty thought?" the reporter says.

JOHN DILLINGER

"My mother had to get a job in a sweatshop making clothes when my father died," Mary says. "She got a hunched back from leaning over a sewing machine all day.

"I worked as a waitress for awhile, and I picked up a few bucks at this nightclub in Kokomo, the Hot Spot. I wore a low-cut blouse and a skirt that was six inches below my navel. I was afraid to sit down, if you know what I mean."

She's a petite woman with red hair and freckled breasts, and she's wearing a red dress and matching shoes.

"I had this red ribbon around my neck that was attached to a tray I carried filled with cigarettes, and the drunken yahoos all thought they could tip me a dime and get a free feel."

"You must have been something, Mary."

She says, "There were thirteen of us kids and we lived in this tenement in Indianapolis. We used old newspapers for rugs, and the halls reeked of corned beef and cabbage, and our clothes came from the Salvation Army. Sometimes I'd go to the mission for the free dinner when there wasn't enough to eat at home, but I got tired of hearing about Jesus."

There's a red sun going down in the sky behind her. It could be a set for a movie.

I say, "I'm planning to break some of our friends out of prison—"

"Jesus."

"—but I'll need your help."

"You've got it, as long as you leave my husband there. Dale said he was going to give me a better life, but the only thing he gave me was crabs."

"What about Pierpont?"

Mary slips her shoes off, then sits on a red sofa, her bare feet on the coffee table in front of her. "I'd do anything to get Harry out."

"Yeah," I say. "He was always talking about you when we were in Michigan City."

All the cons referred to the prison as Michigan City because it didn't have a harsh sound like *state pen*. You could almost imagine it was on the upper peninsula near Mackinaw Island. On a nice day during the summer you could even imagine taking the ferry to the island where you could ride in one of the open carriages pulled by horses because no cars were allowed on the island, and you could feel the breeze blowing across Lake Huron and eat the saltwater taffy they made there.

If you were feeling flush you could stay at the Grand Hotel, where the doormen dressed in red suits and said, "Good day, sir."

It wasn't anything like the Michigan City I spent time at in Indiana. The sand from the dunes to the west stung our faces when we were in the yard and the wind came up in the afternoon.

"Harry always said, 'Mary Kinder is the kindest person I know,' but he says most people's names suit them. He knew a farmer named Drought who lost everything in Oklahoma."

I thought Mary looked like a grown-up Little Red Riding Hood when I first saw her at the prison, but a guard told Harry, "She looks like a whore in her red dress."

"Your mother's a whore," Harry said, then he broke the guard's nose.

They threw Harry into the hole, beating him with baseball bats and batons and rubber hoses, beating him until their arms were too tired to raise their clubs and they gasped for breath. I imagined they joked with one another, laughing, as they saw the purple welts form on his ribs. Someone kicked his genitals as Harry lay on the cement, bleeding from the nose and mouth, pissing blood when he urinated hours later, holding his sides. They had to wash his blood away with a hose.

Each time the guard hit Harry he'd say, "My mother's a whore, is she? Now what do you have to say?"

"Fuck you."

Then the guards would hit him again.

It was eerie, Harry said; he could hear his ribs crack, but it was as if they belonged to someone else as he lay on the cement, bleeding.

When Harry got out of the hole, he took his shoes off and showed us where his toes were grown together—he'd been born that way—and said, "Look what the bastards did to me," and he laughed.

I tell Mary, "I'm supposed to toss a package wrapped in the *Chicago Tribune* into the exercise yard—"

"At least that rag's good for something," Mary says.

"—next to the prison shirt factory the night of the twelfth. The package will have three automatics and eighteen cartridges in it, and I'm smuggling more guns into the shirt factory beneath some bales of material. They'll have so many guns by the time I'm done they'll think they're in a National Guard armory."

"How can I help?" Mary asks.

"You can find them a place they can get to in a hurry—probably Indianapolis—and they'll need new clothes."

43

"Yeah, I can't imagine them parading around Indianapolis in their prison blues. They might look a little suspicious, even to the Polacks," Mary says.

"They're not so bad, Mary. I played baseball with one—"

"Tell me about it. There was this guy named Szymanski who hung around the Hot Spot all the time. He was one of those big tippers who liked to give me the big feel. He said he'd been to this restaurant where you could order fried catfish on the Wabash River. One of the bathrooms was marked with Holes and the other was marked Poles, but Szymanski didn't get it. He scratched his head awhile, then said, 'Jeez, I never been to a place where they had a special crapper for me.'

"Isn't that a good one, Johnnie?" Mary asks, laughing.

"Just be sure you take care of everything," I say. I've never understood prejudice. Even the shines are all right with me.

"You don't have to worry," Mary says. "I'm not Polish."

FALL 1933

I can see the leaves turning color from the window in my bedroom, but Johnnie lies on his back, naked, blowing smoke rings at the ceiling. I can feel the fall sun on my breasts. The afternoons get shorter.

"I got good at it when I was in Michigan City," Johnnie says, blowing another perfect smoke ring. He motions for me to come to him. "There wasn't much else to do."

When I stand next to the bed, he puts his head between my legs, blowing smoke. And I can feel his tongue touching me there. Oh.

"I'll bet you didn't learn that in Michigan City."

Johnnie looks up at me, pleased, then puts his cigarette out in a metal ashtray with a picture of the Empire State Building.

"I never smoked," I say, "but I bought that after I saw the movie about the big ape."

"*King Kong?*"

"Yeah. With Fay Wray. I went to see it every night for a week when it opened here. I cried when all those planes were shooting at Kong and he was on top of the Empire State Building with Fay. You could tell he loved her, but the planes kept buzzing him, shooting, until he fell all the way down into the street. They shouldn't have shot him, Johnnie. He didn't want to hurt anyone."

"Sometimes I think that's the way I'll go," Johnnie says. "They'll just shoot me down in the street like a dog—like Kong."

"You shouldn't talk like that," I say, lying next to him on the bed. "It isn't good to talk that way."

47

JOHN DILLINGER

When I show Marie the photo I took of her sucking her finger in front of the Colonie Nudiste, she laughs. It's a good sound, like rumpled sheets or new money.

In the photo, she's wearing the ring I gave her, displaying it proudly, showing it to everyone. Look. Look. I want to shiver when she tells everyone she's my "honey," but I guess you can get used to anything.

We're lying on her bed, naked, and I show her another photo where she's shaking hands with an organ-grinder's monkey on the boardwalk. The monkey has a sad face, like an old China-man. I'd look sad, too, if I had a leash around my neck.

"Remember that?"

She studies the picture, leaning on her elbows. Her buttocks are alabaster in the light from the window.

"Sure."

The organ-grinder wore a red sultan's hat and the fat seemed to drip from him in the heat. He'd just come to this country from Naples.

The monkey was dressed in a checked vest and faded red pants and it had a hat on, too. It danced while the fat man played the organ. Sometimes it would do a somersault or stick its tongue out and kids would drop a penny into the tin cup the monkey held because they liked to hear it tinkle. I put a dollar in the cup because it was a hell of a way to earn a living.

While we were watching, the cop in the white pith helmet came by. He said, "Get that monkey out of here before it shits on the boardwalk and someone steps in it."

The organ-grinder sweat some more and said, "The monkey's got a rubber diaper on."

"Do tell," the cop said. "I don't care if it's got a banana stuffed up its arse. You ought to put that stinkin' thing in the zoo."

The monkey leaped on top of the organ, curling its lips, biting the organ-grinder on the wrist, then it grabbed the tin cup and circled the boardwalk while the cop yelled, "Why don't you get a decent job?"

The organ-grinder wrapped a handkerchief around his wrist, then picked the monkey up, kissing it, and put it on his shoulder.

"You must be crazy to kiss the filthy beast after it bit you. I ought to run you in for bein' a lunatic," the cop said, but the organ-grinder had already headed down the boardwalk. His shoes seemed too big for his feet.

I tell Marie, "He kind of reminded me of Charlie Chaplin," then I sit up in bed, listening.

"Do you hear it?"

"What?" Marie asks.

"Footsteps. Someone talking."

"You're probably imagining things," Marie says, but she cocks her head like the RCA dog. "It's all right. It's Mrs. Stricker, the landlady."

"Were you expecting her?"

"She's probably talking to the old guy across the hall. They're always getting together for pinochle."

Before I can get out of bed, someone kicks Marie's door in, and two men enter the apartment, the door banging against the wall. It's a hell of an entrance.

One of them's holding a sawed-off shotgun and the other's holding a submachine gun.

The door's hanging on one hinge.

I tell Marie, "I don't think they're here to play pinochle," and she pulls the sheet over her breasts.

"What're you gawking at?" she asks, but they're not looking at her.

A woman wearing a babushka and a faded blue house-dress stands in the hall behind them. She's a crone.

The guy with the sawed-off shotgun says, "Stick 'em up, John. We're police officers."

"So where're your badges?"

"I don't need a goddamn badge as long as I've got this," the guy holding the Thompson says. "You want to argue?"

I get out of bed, holding my hands up, naked.

"I don't have nothing to hide," I say.

CHARLES E. GROSS

When Pfauhl and I bring Dillinger to the station he says, "Foul and Gross, what beautiful names."

"It's pronounced *Fall*," my partner says. *"Fall."*

"Sorry."

"I bet."

"I didn't know if you were part of another gang or not. It's hard to tell with plainsclothesmen. I thought you might be some-body else."

Pfauhl says, "We found a thirty-eight under the sofa cushion in the broad's apartment and several other guns in your luggage, along with two thousand, six hundred and four dollars in cash. Why were you carrying so much money?"

"You never know when you might want to take a vaca-tion," Dillinger says. He smiles, lighting a cigarette.

"There were several rounds of ammunition and some roofing nails in your Essex," I say. "What are you doing with all that?"

I know what he was doing.

Dillinger says, "I was going to help Dad fix the roof on the barn, then we were going to go hunting. Is there a law against that?"

"There is if you're using a Thompson to do it," I say.

"I wanted to make sure I wouldn't miss."

Pfauhl says, "You weren't planning to rob a bank by any chance?"

"I think you've been reading too many detective novels," Dillinger says.

RUSSELL K. PFAUHL

Gross and I go into the john when we've finished with Dillinger.

We stand next to one another at the urinals. The room smells of chlorine and tobacco, and I wonder why anyone would want to smoke in the john.

"Jesus, did you see the schlong on that guy when he got out of bed?" Gross asks, shaking his dick.

"How could I miss?"

"He's hung like an elephant."

"Yeah, I wonder how it feels for the women."

"I guess you'd have to ask the broad he was with," Gross says.

HARRY PIERPONT

"It's ironic," Mary says.

"Yeah. Ironic."

Mary's always reading books. She says there isn't much else to do when you're waiting for someone to get out of stir, but I think she'd read the print on a box of mush if she didn't have a book.

I don't know what she's talking about half the time.

There're books all over her place, but she particularly likes gangster novels. She claims they help her understand the way I live.

I don't know. I never read one.

"Johnnie set everything up, but he gets arrested four days before you and the boys got out. It's like he had a bad karma or something."

"Yeah. Bad karma."

Makley, Red, and I made it to Mary's place the day the cops caught up with Marie Longnaker's brother, Jimmy, in Bean-blossom. He was coming out of the bathroom at a Standard Oil station, wiping his hands, when the state police opened fire.

I wonder if he had a bad karma.

I tell Mary, "I wanted to kill the captain of the day watch before we broke out, but Makley kept telling me, 'No, no. You gotta use your head. If you shoot him now we'll have every guard in the joint comin' for us, and we'll never get out of here.'

"The cap was this big guy, two or three inches over six feet, and he must have weighed three hundred pounds. We called him 'Big Bertha,' and he was responsible for most of the beatings I got. When I jammed my pistol into the bastard's fat stomach, I could feel him quivering.

"It reminded me of a Christmas poem my mother read me when I was a kid. Something about Santa Claus having a stomach like a bowl full of jelly. That's what Cap's was like, but he wasn't Santa. I told him, 'I wish you'd give me a reason to blow a hole in your fat guts so I can watch them leak out,' but he didn't say nothin'. Not a word. He just went across the yard with the ten of us to the main gate. I told Cap, 'You're lucky this time,' then I hit him with the butt of my pistol, and the ten of us were running through the front gates."

Makley, Red, and I stayed together because we'd all worked in the machine shop and knew each other.

Makley was a funny little guy who looked like a bank

president. He was slow-moving, and he walked around with his stomach stickin' out like a little king. When he was younger, he'd worked as a railroad switchman in Detroit but he said, "Watchin' all them trains coming and goin' made me feel like I was standin' still. Everyone was goin' someplace but me. That's when I decided I needed a new career." He'd tried selling used cars for Horse Trader Ed in Detroit, but he liked bank robbing better.

It had begun to rain by the time we came to a gas station near the prison. There was a mechanic working on an Essex Terraplane.

Red told him, "I'll blow your fuckin' brains out if you don't give us the keys," but the fool said, "Go ahead, buddy," and ran off into the rain.

I didn't get it.

The Terraplane didn't belong to the mechanic, and he wouldn't be able to afford one if he worked at the crummy gas station a thousand years.

What was it to him?

Makley pushed Red's arm down before he could fire and said, "It's all right."

"What do you mean, 'It's all right'? He's runnin' away with the fuckin' keys and we're standing here in the rain with our fingers up our ass."

"At least you only got three of them," Makley said.

The index and middle fingers of Red's right hand were missing. He had a chunky build, but he was always skipping rope in Michigan City. His dark red hair was going gray around the edges, and he had a perpetual frown. Maybe he missed his two fingers.

"Why don't you just shut the fuck up?" Red asked.

"Horse Trader Ed taught me something," Makley said. "Besides patience, that is. It always takes patience to make a deal."

"Fuck Horse Trader Ed."

"He wore a cowboy suit and claimed he was born too late. He was always talkin' about how he wanted to meet Tom Mix. Instead of sellin' used cars, Ed said he should of been ridin' the Chisholm Trail, but it had been paved over with concrete by the time he was grown up. Ol' Ed could hot-wire any car on the lot in less than thirty seconds, and he taught me how," Makley said, reaching under the dashboard. "It was the only honest job I ever had where I learned something useful."

Makley drove west on State Route 12, heading toward Gary in the hard rain. He said, "The cops will expect us to head toward Indianapolis, but we can get some new clothes and another car in Gary before we go south. It's a fun town. I know this place where a woman dances with no clothes, and she has this boa constrictor—"

"I don't like snakes," Red said.

"The first time I seen her dance, I thought it was going to crawl up her snatch."

The windshield wipers couldn't push the rain away fast enough, but Makley didn't slow down. His chin was almost resting on the wheel he leaned over so far, trying to see the highway.

"For Christ sake, slow down," Red said. "You're doin' eighty."

"Why don't you quit complaining?" Makley said. "I thought you were in a hurry."

We stole another car that was parked in front of an old hotel with peeling white paint and a weathercock that spun crazily in the wind above the entrance when we drove through Ogden Dunes.

We hid the Terraplane in some woods at the edge of town. It was late afternoon, but lights were already on in all the farmhouses. Inside, people were probably going on with their dreary lives while they listened to Tom Mix on the radio or caught up on the comics from last Sunday. Little Orphan Annie was probably telling the poor schmucks, "Ya hafta earn what ya get."

Not if you robbed banks, you didn't.

"I hate it when Little Orphan Annie says 'Leapin' Lizards,'" I said.

"I think there's somethin' funny goin' on between her and Daddy Warbucks," Red said.

"I think you got a perverted mind," Makley said. "She's just a kid."

We could feel the rear end of the Ford slide when Makley cornered too fast, but I didn't say anything. I felt a lot safer in the Terraplane.

It was still raining when we got ourselves a room at a cheap hotel—you could rent rooms by the hour or the night—and we bought some used clothes at a thrift shop where the old lady who ran it was hard of hearing. Later, Mary said we'd done her job for her.

We had T-bone steaks at this diner that was built in the shadow of the steel mills. We could see the flames shooting from the chimneys at the mill while we ate. It was almost nine and the cook had on a local radio station. We were the only ones in the place.

The announcer said, "Here we are, folks, right on the scene of a gigantic manhunt. The troops are lined up all around here. There go more squads through that field of death, right on the trail of the felons. The troops claim Pierpont and Makley are in the woods across those fields."

"What about me?" Red asked. "Where am I supposed to be?"

"Shut up," Makley said. There was a lot of static.

"Listen closely now, folks, and you can hear the shots as a deadly patter of lead is rained all about. Oh, boy, this is exciting. What a battle."

The cook spit on the grill and said, "Jeez." He was wearing a greasy white hat and apron.

I tell Mary, "You could hear machine guns and pistols being fired. They were mixed with the rain and sirens and the screams of a woman. She kept saying, 'They got 'em, they got 'em.'

"'What the hell is a broad doin' there?' Red asked.

"I told him I thought the whole thing was a fake, that the announcer was making it all up. And I was right. The captain of the state police, Matt Leach, wanted to have the announcer arrested the next day, but Leach didn't know what to charge him with so the cops settled for a retraction."

Mary says, "I wish they were lying about capturing Johnnie."

"Yeah, that would sure make things a lot easier," I say.

JOHN DILLINGER

There're men with machine guns stationed on the roof of the county jail in Dayton, waiting for me to make a break.

"They must think I'm a dangerous man," I say.

"I wonder what gave them that idea," Gross says. His nose is crooked, as if someone broke it in a fight and it wasn't set properly, and his eyes remind me of a turtle's. He always looks sleepy.

He's slumped behind the wheel of the Buick as we pull out of the prison. Pfauhl's sitting behind me. I can feel the barrel of his .38 against the back of my neck.

"I hope we don't hit a bump in the road," I say. They're transferring me to the Allen County Jail in Lima.

"If we do, you won't know about it," Pfauhl says.

"Yeah, there'll just be this big boom and it'll all be over,"

Gross says, laughing. Before we left the prison, he cuffed my hands behind my back.

"Where're the leg irons?" I asked.

"We left them in the torture chamber," Gross said.

I slump against the seat, trying to get comfortable, but it's impossible.

"You don't mind if I call you Chuck, do you? It has a nicer ring to it than Gross."

"I don't care what you call me."

"Just don't call him Chuckie," Pfauhl says. "He hates Chuckie."

"I kind of like Chuckie," I say.

We drive through a small town named Hardin, and I watch a farmer wearing a plaid jacket burn cornstalks in a field next to the road. The smoke curls into the air like a question mark. You can tell it's fall. I say, "We must be in outlaw territory, Chuckie."

"What're you talkin' about?" Pfauhl asks. I can still feel his .38 against the back of my neck.

"John Wesley Hardin was one of the great pistoleers of the Old West."

"What the hell is a pistoleer?" Gross asks.

"A gunfighter. Hardin was supposed to be the deadliest man in Texas."

"If he's so famous, how come I never heard of him?"

"Maybe you skipped school that day."

"Yeah, I must have."

There's a sign at the edge of McCartyville saying, WE LOVE OUR CHILDREN. DRIVE SAFELY.

Gross says, "They probably hate the little bastards," and he speeds up as he passes a one-room schoolhouse that's painted barn red and an Esso station. An old darky wearing a ruined derby is leaning against the pumps, his hands in his pockets, waiting for nothing. I'd wave at him if my hands weren't cuffed.

"Did you ever hear of Henry McCarty?" I ask.

"Sure, he's the mayor of this dump," Gross says.

"Maybe you heard of Billy the Kid," I say. "That was his name, Henry McCarty."

"You don't know nothin'." Gross lights a cigarette, blowing smoke in my face. "You're as dumb as that nigger back there. The Kid's name was William Bonney, and he killed twenty-one men by the time he was twenty-one and that sheriff shot him."

"Yeah, you don't know nothin'," Pfauhl says, jamming his pistol into the back of my neck. "You gotta learn to keep your mouth shut."

HARRY PIERPONT

Makley, Red, and I watch the Columbus Day Parade after we drive by the Allen County Jail a few times. It ought to be easy, breaking John out, but we want to wait till it's dark. The sheriff says John's "just another punk," and Sarber's refused additional security.

I stand on the curb between Makley and Red, clapping when the Lima High School Band and the majorettes go by, twirling their batons.

I used to play clarinet. The band instructor thought I was good enough to turn professional, but I became a pro at something else. Sometimes I wonder if I made the right choice.

I say, "I love a parade."

There're more bands, a clown on a unicycle, some bagpipers, and the mayor of Lima rides by, smiling and waving, in an open roadster. People live and die in these little towns. I think they believe the earth is flat—that they'd fall off it if they ever left the county. A blonde in a blue bathing suit throws confetti to the crowd.

"Look at the tits on that babe," Red says.

"You got tits on the brain," Makley says. "She's probably in the tenth grade."

"At least I don't get my kicks watchin' a naked woman let a snake crawl up her snatch."

"It didn't crawl up her snatch," Makley says.

We have pork chops and mashed potatoes with runny gravy at a place called the Chicken Shack; Red burps and says, "I think we should of had the fried chicken."

I think so, too.

It's 6:15 when Red parks the Terraplane in front of the jail. He leaves the engine running while Makley and I go inside.

The sheriff's sitting behind his desk, reading a paper, while his wife works a crossword puzzle. Across the room, the deputy's playing with a brown dog. The cells are through a barred doorway across the room. I used to think I wanted a life like that: a wife, maybe a couple of kids, and a dog.

I could do without the deputy.

Sarber sets the *Lima News* down, looking at us. His revolver's in a holster hanging from a peg on the wall, and I can see the deputy's pistol and cartridge belt on his desk.

I say, "We're officers from Michigan City—here to question John Dillinger."

"Let me see your credentials," Sarber says. His bald head gleams in the light.

I pull my .45 from a shoulder holster and say, "Here's my credentials," and Makley pulls his .38.

"You can't do that," Sarber says. He gets up, pushing his chair back, reaching for his pistol.

"No, don't," I say, pulling the trigger.

I shoot him twice, watching the blood blossom onto his

shirt and pants as he falls backward. Watching his life leak away. Some people just don't understand what *no* means. Sarber's body makes a muffled sound, like a bale of hay hitting the ground.

I used to buck hay.

Makley says, "Give us the keys to the cells," bringing the butt of his pistol down so hard Sarber's scalp is split open to the bone.

"Don't kill him," Mrs. Sarber says. Her pale blue eyes are watery, and her lower lip quivers.

The deputy's standing next to his desk with his hands up. He's wearing a hat that would look better on a milkman.

"Then give us the keys—now."

Mrs. Sarber hands them to me, then Makley motions her and the deputy to sit on the floor, facing him, along the far wall. The dog sits next to them, licking Mrs. Sarber's hand, when I open the door to the cell block.

John's putting his coat on, grinning.

"I heard the shots," he says, then he shakes hands with one of the prisoners. "You sure you don't want to come along?" he asks. I almost expect him to sign autographs before we leave.

"Nah, I don't have much time to do, but good luck to you."

I tell the other men, "Get back. We just want John."

When we go into Sarber's office, he's lying on the floor, moaning. He keeps saying, "Men, why'd you do this to me?"

"You shouldn't have acted stupid," I say.

I hand John a pistol, then Makley and I lock Mrs. Sarber and the deputy in the cell block. She kept saying, "Please, let me stay with my husband. I think Jess is dying," but she'd be out the door, screaming, the second we took off.

Sarber says, "Turn me over on my side. My back hurts."

John says, "I'm sorry Jess. You were okay to me, but you shouldn't have tried to stop them."

We can hear some Legionnaires partying down the street

when we go outside. One of them staggers toward us. He stands, swaying, in front of John, studying his face. "Don't I know you?"

"Maybe you saw my picture in the paper."

"Yeah, that must be it," the Legionnaire says. "I really like your movies," then he staggers down the street.

John's smiling when we get into the car.

Red says, "I heard shots."

"I had to shoot Sheriff Sarber."

"You guys get to have all the fun," Red says.

JOHN DILLINGER

Billie and I can hear them singing "Happy birthday, dear Harry" down the hall at his parents' farmhouse. I know they must be cutting the cake by now, toasting each other with champagne they'll drink out of jelly glasses. Harry's mother loves to make apple jelly.

Billie and I sit on the edge of the bed, naked. I think I've spent a third of my life sitting on strange beds in back rooms with women I hardly know, but it's not a bad way to pass the time.

I met Billie when she was working as a waitress at John Barleycorn's in Chicago. She told me she was half-French and half-Menominee Indian, and I touched her cheek while we stood next to the bar. I'd never met anyone with such smooth skin.

"I'd like a tequila sunrise," she said.

"I didn't think they allowed Indians to have firewater."

"It's all right. It's the French half of me that drinks."

I watch Billie fasten her bra as we sit on the edge of the bed. She has small, fragile-looking breasts. She touches them gently and says, "They're always softer after I make love. I wonder why," but I don't think she expects an answer.

There're so many things I don't know.

Then she touches her stomach, as if it too were softer.

"I'm glad we got away for a few minutes, Johnnie. Parties give me a headache."

"It's Harry's father." His whining nasal voice followed us down the hall. "I think he was vaccinated with a phonograph needle."

"Yeah, but he and his wife mean well. You notice how they keep saying, 'Harry never done a wrong thing in his life?'"

"I wonder what they'll say when they learn about Sheriff Sarber."

"They'll probably make some kind of excuse, but I like that about them. My mother never thought I did anything right. I ran away from home when I was thirteen."

I pull my shorts on and go over to the cold window. The floorboards squeak as I cross the room. The wallpaper's peeling and there's a stain on the ceiling where the roof probably leaked. The brass bedstead's tarnished and Washington must have slept on the mattress, but it's comfortable.

I look out across the dark fields, past the apple orchard, wondering where Marie went. She disappeared when her brother was killed.

Billie came to me as if she were a gift. I watch her comb her long black hair as I button my shirt.

Someone embroidered the words GOD BLESS OUR HOME on a doily and put it in a cheap frame that hangs crookedly over the bed.

Billie touches up her lipstick while I finish dressing. Then I straighten the frame because there're enough crooked things in my life.

"We'd better get back to the party," I tell Billie.

RED HAMILTON

It's almost midnight when Makley pulls up in front of the cop station in Auburn. It's a dirty red-brick building across from the court-house, and the guy who designed it must have liked ugly things.

"I hate these late hours," Makley says.

"Maybe you should find another line of work."

"I don't know how to do nothin' else."

"Then quit complaining."

John and I get out of the car, straightening our jackets. There's a pale yellow light coming through the window of the main office, but everything else is dark.

John decided we need more guns, ammunition, and some bulletproof vests if we're going to stay in business. "It's called an investment in the future," he said. "You have to acquire the tools you need."

"So where're we gonna get all these guns?" Harry asked. He got belligerent when he drank too much, and he'd been drinking all evening. He turned thirty-two last night, and he was worried about losing his good looks.

"We'll visit a friendly cop station," John said.

"And then what? Say, 'Pretty please, we'd like a couple of Thompsons, a sawed-off shotgun and a few revolvers.' Maybe we could say, 'Mother, may I?'"

He leaned against his girlfriend. Mary called him Hand-some Harry, and she was the only thing that kept him from falling down last night. I don't think he's so special-looking.

John and I take our pistols out.

I say, "I think it's a great idea."

"Yeah, I'm a natural-born leader." He smiles. "It'll be a great idea if it works. You can congratulate me when we're out of here."

Two cops are sitting at their desks when John and I go into the main office. One's stuffing his face from a greasy brown-paper sack filled with popcorn, and the other's eyes are heavy.

John points his .45 at the sleepy-looking cop and says,

"We don't want to shoot anyone unless we have to. We just want the key to your gun cabinet."

"It's over there," the sleepy cop says, pointing toward a ring of keys hanging from the coatrack. His name's Krueger, and he likes to beat up on drunks and little guys.

"I've heard about you for years," I say. He has thinning blond hair and a sallow complexion.

"Is that a fact?"

"Yeah, it's a true fact."

John keeps him covered while I take his gun away.

The other cop just sits there, holding his greasy sack of popcorn. He has three chins and they're all greasy, too. I take away his pistol, then lock him and Krueger in a cell while John opens the gun cabinet.

Before I leave the cell block the greasy cop says, "What about my popcorn?"

"I'll leave it on your desk," I say. "What do you think I am, a thief?" then I go back into the office and help John clean the cabinet out.

There's a Thompson submachine gun, a shotgun, two rifles, six pistols, three bulletproof vests, and more than a thousand rounds of ammunition.

"I think I died and went to heaven," John says, loading the arsenal into our car.

"Hallelujah," I say.

MARY KINDER

Harry sits on the porch swing at his parents' farmhouse. His hands shake, holding a cup of coffee that's getting cold.

"You don't look too good," I say, listening to an owl hoot from the loft of the barn. I wonder why they call outlaws *owlhoots*.

"Thanks for reminding me," Harry says.

It's cold on the porch. Harry's wearing a leather jacket and I'm wearing the mink coat he got me. I wish he'd take me someplace nice where I could show it off, but he says he has to keep a low profile. He told me, "People like us walk in darkness." I thought it was a funny thing to say.

Johnnie takes Billie places.

"I should have gone on the job with them," Harry says.

The chain on the swing squeaks as we move, and the moon's almost hidden by the clouds. Someone in a book called the moon *obfuscated* when it looks like this. I had to look the word up, but I liked it.

"You said it was a dumb idea to rob a cop station last night."

"I was drunk last night."

"I noticed."

"It doesn't matter if it's a dumb idea. I'm part of the gang. I'm supposed to be there."

"Everybody gets a day off. Maybe your day off is Saturday."

"Yeah," Harry says, but he looks morose.

I sit on the swing next to him. I can hear the radio playing in the kitchen. Someone's singing "You can't get away from me."

I don't want to get away.

"Three thousand people showed up for the funeral of that sheriff you shot. They buried him this afternoon. I heard about it on the radio."

"I don't care where you heard it."

"Captain Leach, head of the Indiana state police, even went to Ohio for the funeral. He called the Dillinger Gang a bunch of mad dogs."

"That's because John sent him a book titled *How to Be a Detective.*"

"Did he really?"

"Yeah, why would I make somethin' like that up?"

"I don't know . . . It's funny."

"Leach didn't think so."

I lean against Harry's shoulder, looking at the obfuscated moon. "The announcer said Sarber got full military honors."

"I don't care what he got. He was a fool, going for his pistol."

"I guess you didn't have any choice," I say.

EMMETT HANCOCK

I'm sawing wood, stacking it next to the side of the house, when someone drives up in a new Ford. He gets out of the car, slamming the door shut with a backhanded flip of his wrist. You can tell he thinks he's clever.

He takes a notebook out of his shirt pocket and says, "Can I talk to you about your brother-in-law?"

People always want to talk about John.

"Seems like you already have your mind made up," I say. "What happens if I say no?"

"I'd keep coming back. Or someone else would. So why don't you just talk to me now and save everyone a lot of time?"

"I'm all for saving time." I lean against the sawhorse. "There's a lot of getting ready for winter. The corn has to be shucked and the wood must be cut."

The reporter rests one foot on the running board, like he's waiting to have his picture took. He probably has one of them horns that go *ooga ooga*. He's a hotshot, all right.

He says, "Tell me about John."

"I'm all for him. That's not to say I'm upholding him in any of his crimes. That is, if he committed any."

"He's sure wanted for robbing a lot of banks."

"I don't know why the law should want him or anyone else for bank robbery. He isn't half as bad as a crooked banker or a crooked politician because he gives the bankers a chance to fight, and they never give people a chance. John doesn't rob poor people. If he robs anyone, he robs them who became rich by robbing the poor."

"A regular Robin Hood, huh?" The reporter adjusts the brim of his hat. "Tell me, what was he like when he was a kid?"

"He loved baseball and was a good all-around ballplayer. He was a good batter, good fielder, and fast—he could steal anything, so they said."

"He sure proved them right about that," the reporter says.

PENNY HANCOCK

The last of the trick-or-treaters have gone, and my parents have been in bed for an hour when someone knocks at the back door. It's almost midnight, and I'm listening to a disk jockey from Indianapolis, trying to study for an English exam. The black coffee doesn't seem to help. I hum along with the song "Sweet Adeline."

No one ever comes to the kitchen door, except for a few hobos offering to do some chore for a hot meal. They'll stand there, dirty and tattered, like some scruffy character from Oz, holding their hats. You can tell they wouldn't be much good at anything. All they really want is a handout.

Daddy's already cut and stacked the wood for winter so there isn't much for a hobo to do, but Mom always gives them something. She says not everyone is as lucky as we are.

When I open the door, I almost expect to see the raven Poe wrote about, but it's my Uncle Johnnie.

"Trick or treat."

"I thought you were a dark bird."

I can tell the young woman with him wonders why I expected a bird to be at the door, but she has the good manners not to ask.

I feel like a fool.

Uncle Johnnie tells me the woman's name is Billie when they come into the kitchen. He's wearing a raccoon coat and Billie's is mink, but she's casual about it, draping it over the back of a chair. They could be the beautiful people in a Fitzgerald novel, standing there, rubbing their hands together before the woodstove in the corner.

He says, "Billie and I are headed for Chicago, but I wanted to stop by the farm and say good-bye to Dad before we leave. This is about the only time I can do it."

I turn the radio off and pour them black coffee in a tin cup and an Ovaltine mug, and we sit around the kitchen table, like members of a normal family. I know Johnnie and his gang have stolen guns and ammunition from two police stations, along with robbing banks in Greencastle and South Bend, in less than two weeks. Governor McNutt has called out the National Guard.

Anything Uncle Johnnie does is all right with me.

He lights cigarettes for himself and Billie, then he leans back in the chair, balancing it on two legs, his feet in the air before him. He always was a show-off. He blows a perfect smoke ring and smiles. "I thought you might like to come to the farm with us . . . if you don't have too much homework."

"Sure."

I leave a note for my parents on the kitchen table in case they wake up while I'm gone, then I put on my coat and the three of us go out into the yard. The snow's coming down soft and fine like ground cornmeal.

Billie says, "I'll get in back," when we reach the car.

We head down the lane toward the main road. I've never ridden in a car at midnight with a machine gun on my lap. It was on the front seat and I didn't know where else to put it.

"They always work you that hard at that college you go to?" Johnnie asks. "Or did you just put off doing your homework?" He steers with one hand. "I always put mine off as long as possible when I was in school. There were always so many other things to do that were more interesting." He laughs, gesturing with his free hand. "Look where it got me."

I like it when he laughs. I remember him laughing when we wrestled on the front-room floor of my parents' house and I'd tickle him. Uncle Johnnie always let me win.

"You're the most famous bank robber in America," Billie says. You can tell she's proud.

"Yeah, and I have to sneak into my hometown at midnight if I don't want to get shot."

"Every job has its ups and downs, I suppose."

Johnnie's quiet for a moment, then he turns to me. His face is pale in the moonlight. "Do you have a special beau?"

He doesn't seem to think it's strange for me to be cradling the machine gun. Probably his friends do it all the time. I guess you get used to anything.

"No, I'm waiting for someone like you to come along."

"Someone who robs banks?"

"Sure, I could be the gun moll, and my beau and I could join up with the Dillinger Gang." I like to tease him. "Or with Bonnie Parker and Clyde Barrow."

"Barrow's a punk," Johnnie says.

"Definitely, the Dillinger Gang then. I don't hang out with punks."

"Good for you," Billie says. "I met a lot of punks in my life, including one I married, and they were all bad news. Stay away from punks."

"I'd have to learn how to use one of these if I joined your gang," I say, hefting the machine gun.

I roll the window down, pointing the Thompson at the signs we speed past in the darkness, *"Rat-a-tat-tat, rat-a-tat-tat,"* then I turn toward Uncle Johnnie. "Do gangsters really say things like, 'Take that, you dirty rat?' Or is that just something they say in the movies?"

"I never called anyone a rat," he says, "but I knew a few."

I lean out the window, feeling the fine snow hit my face. I yell into the wind, "I'll take care of the coppers!" and imagine I'm spraying lead at them. *"Rat-a-tat-tat, rat-a-tat-tat."* It's all very dramatic. "Take that."

Uncle Johnnie's laughter fills the car as we head down the dark road toward the farm, the snow swirling in the headlights.

JOHN DILLINGER

"Where's Mary?" I ask.

Harry's sitting at the kitchen table, reading the morning paper. I don't know why. The news is always lousy.

Harry shrugs. "How should I know?"

"What happened to breakfast?"

"Mary got tired of fixing breakfast."

"Tired?"

"Yeah."

I pour a cup of coffee and sit across the table from Harry. Four of us rented a six-room flat on the third floor.

"I thought everything was going fine."

"Yeah. It was fine for you and Billie. The two of you spend all your time sleepin' while Mary's in here getting everything ready. Mary says she don't even have time to comb her hair, but Billie comes out lookin' like a princess every mornin'. Mary says it ain't right. She's goin' on strike."

"I never heard of a cook going on strike."

"Maybe she's forming a cook's union." Harry leans back in his chair, smiling.

"I thought we made a deal. Mary would do the cooking and you and I would look around for another bank."

"What was Billie supposed to do? Look beautiful?"

"Why not? She's good at it."

"Yeah, Mary says she must be good at a lot of things. It's too bad cookin' ain't one of them."

I've never had a bed partner like Billie, but that's not any of Harry's business. The men I know who brag about their sex lives spend all their time listening to the radio.

"Mary says Billie comes out smellin' like lemon water every morning, but it takes Mary an hour to get the smell of potatoes and rashers out of her hair." Harry leans forward, frowning. "What's *rashers?*"

"Damned if I know."

I go into the bedroom, awakening Billie. I watch her rub the sleep from her large brown eyes.

"Mary's gone on strike," I say.

BILLIE FRECHETTE

John winks at me as he picks up the telephone. "I've got to make a long-distance call."

"My father always used to talk about long distance. Then, one day, he was gone. My mother got a card from him later. It was postmarked Paris."

"Why would he want to go to Texas?"

"Paris, France. I told you I'm half-French." I can see the clouds swirling like cotton candy over Lake Michigan. The sky's crimson, and I know it will be dark soon. "The card had a one-sentence message: 'Good-bye.' We never heard from him again."

John picks up the receiver, saying, "Operator, I'd like long distance," then he gives her a number, and I imagine a phone ringing somewhere faraway in another room where the people come and go.

I dreamt about long distance after my father left. The card he sent had a picture of a bridge and the words *Pont Neuf*, and you could see the Cathedral of Notre Dame in the distance. I didn't know what Pont Neuf meant, but I knew the Seine was a river that ran through Paris.

My father always had a flair for life, and I imagined him wandering the streets wearing a beret and drinking Pernod in small cafés where the gingham tablecloths had red-and-white squares.

I try to make a church with my fingers. It was a game we played as children, before my father went away. This is the church and this is the steeple. Open the door and look at the people.

"Hello . . . I'd like to speak to Captain Matt Leach," John says, then he sips a beer I poured him, waiting.

"Leach? How are you, you stuttering bastard? This is John Dillinger. I thought the book I sent you on *How to Be a Detective* might help, but you're not even close enough to eat my dust." Then John hangs the phone up, laughing.

CAPTAIN MATT LEACH

"Ga . . . get me John Dillinger, da . . . dead or alive."

HARRY PIERPONT

"You got to face it, John. You're not a movie star. You go into a bank with a job to do, like a plumber with his tool kit. But your tools consist of a forty-five and a Thompson. Other than that, there ain't any difference between us. But you don't get it. You think you gotta go into a bank like Elmo Lincoln."

"I kind of had Douglas Fairbanks in mind," John says.

"You think you gotta leap over the counter like Tarzan, that you gotta show off all the time, like you did in Greencastle. You're gonna get us all killed doin' that."

"We walked out of there with seventy-five thousand dollars. I wouldn't complain too much. You didn't mind taking your share of the money."

"You remind me of Babe Ruth during that World Series game last year. It's the fifth inning and Charlie Root's pitchin' for the Cubs—"

"I know who was pitching."

"—and the fuckin' Babe takes two strikes from Charlie. Then the Babe points to the bleachers to show the crowd where the next pitch is gonna go. And, wham!" I swing my arms, holding an empty beer bottle like it's a bat. "The Babe takes the pitch and knocks the ball into the bleachers."

"He got the job done, didn't he?"

"Yeah, but did he have to be such a fuckin' show-off?"

JOHN DILLINGER

Billie leans over me, sucking my penis, her mouth filled with white wine. It gives me a giddy feeling, like going into a bank and leaping over the counter, one hand on the partition, the other holding a gun.

I felt this way once when I stuck my cock into an apple a neighbor girl had hollowed out for me when we were teens. Apple juice ran down my balls and she licked them and said, "Oh, Johnnie, it's like apple cider." "If you say so."

It was summer and she wore a yellow sundress. She said she wanted to save herself for her future husband so we didn't make love, but she let me put a finger into her tight little hole.

We were in the field behind her parents' house, and I masturbated, spreading my seed into the hot furrows where we lay, because she wanted to watch. I don't remember her name, but I remember my sperm glistened when she held a drop of it on her finger in the noonday sun.

Billie straddles me, and I slide into her as she leans forward, her breasts like inverted bells.

She told me her leg hurts during the winter, but she moves easily now. She says, "I didn't know lovemaking could be so therapeutic," and she smiles when I ask her what that means. "Good for you."

Billie, I never thought I'd feel this good again.

I massage the contours of her breasts, touching her nipples, as we move together. She wants to move to California because she heard you can reach out your window, plucking an orange, and her leg wouldn't hurt in the warm weather. "Imagine that, Johnnie, plucking an orange from your own tree," and I imagine walking, naked, in a warm rain in Los Angeles.

Billie's breasts are like oranges, and the orange light comes into the room.

Some people say coming is a little death, but I've never

believed that. I've come in a hundred hotel rooms, in the backseats of cars, under a full moon, in that field behind the girl's house where I called myself Johnnie Appleseed, and I've come watching Sally Rand do her fan dance. I've said, "I'm coming," when I was with Marie and the cops knocked on her door. I've come in phone booths, listening to a woman's voice on the receiver, and a young lady gave me a hand job on the el train while I pretended to read the paper, coming.

Billie rests her head on my chest and says, "I can hear your heart beating; it's a friendly heart. 'Billie,' it's saying, 'Billie.'"

BILLIE FRECHETTE

I park the Terraplane across the street from the doctor's office. John and I watch a few cars go by, grinding their way through the slush. Most people are home by now. Home.

All I had was a shack on the reservation and some cheap rooms where the furnace never seemed to work until I met John, but we're always moving. Our apartments may be expensive, but they have as much personality as flypaper. Maybe John and I can settle down. Someday.

It's the coldest November 15th in Chicago's history, and people hurry home in the darkness, their feet sliding. They could be dancing on the snow and ice. I'm wearing fur-lined gloves, but my fingers feel frozen.

John ought to take up bank robbing in California.

"You'd think someone named Dr. Eye would be an optometrist," I say.

"Why?"

"Because he should be an 'eye' doctor, not a dermatologist." I laugh. "Get it?"

"Oh, yeah."

I can tell he doesn't think it's funny. Maybe I wouldn't, either, if I were being treated for ringworm. John said he got it when he was in the Allen County Jail.

John watches the street.

It's 7:15, and he has a 7:30 appointment.

"See anything?"

"Nothing special."

The light's on in Dr. Eye's office, and the drugstore below is still open. I can see a man wearing a white smock moving around behind the prescription counter, and I wonder what it would be like to push pills ten or twelve hours a day. I've heard people who work those hours say they're lucky to have a job, lucky not to be out on the street selling apples or begging, "Brother, can you spare a dime."

Some luck.

They won't get any competition from me. That's for sure. They spend their lives getting up and going to work and coming home. If they're lucky, they get to listen to *Amos and Andy* on the radio.

Some luck.

John watches the street closely.

A kid tries to hawk the evening news. He waves a paper, yelling, "Extry, extry," but no one seems to care. People hurry by him, the collars on their coats up, their frozen breath in the air. They know the news; people are dying from the cold.

A Chinese restaurant has a sign in the window saying WHITE TRADE ONLY, and I laugh. "Can you imagine a Chinese restaurant turning a Chink away?"

"Maybe they consider themselves white."

"They must be color-blind if they do."

"Maybe they should get an 'eye' exam," John says.

He tucks a .45 into his shoulder holster, then drops a snub-nosed .38 into his coat pocket.

I watch John cross the street as an elevated train rattles by in the distance, and the snow swirls around him. The tails of his overcoat flap in the wind.

A car with Indiana plates passes me slowly as John goes up the dimly-lit stairwell to Dr. Eye's office.

The streetlights have halos around them, but I almost expect them to shatter, like a thermometer exploding from the cold.

People die in weather like this.

Two squad cars round the corner, coming toward me. One of them parks on the wrong side of the street, facing me, about seventy-five feet away, and the other passes me slowly, like the car from Indiana. The cops stare at me as they drive by.

Oh oh.

Something's wrong.

JOHN DILLINGER

Dr. Eye finishes my exam, then he stands next to the bay windows, gazing down at the street. He's a tall, wiry man in his mid-forties. He might have been a long-distance runner when he was younger.

"Look at all the police cars out there," he says. "I wonder what happened."

I can see Billie silhouetted behind the wheel of the Terraplane when I go to the windows. A cop car passes her slowly in the swirling snow.

I remember Frank James said he got tired of seeing Judas on the face of every friend he had, that he got tired of night-riding and day-hiding, of constantly listening for footfalls and creaking doors.

I'm tired, too

Where are you, Judas Iscariot? Who are you?

I give Dr. Eye a ten-dollar bill, telling him, "Keep the change," then I run down the stairs and out onto the street, a pistol in each hand.

Some guns flash in the darkness, then I hear the bullets thud into the building behind me. I fire two shots at one of the cop cars, running across the street, then I jump into the Terraplane.

Billie backs up, ramming a police car, while I grab the machine gun from the backseat. The radiator on the car Billie hit is steaming, and the steam rises, mixing with the snow. It could be a scene from *Dracula,* but there's no castle in the background, only Dr. Eye's office and the strange fog and a barber sitting in one of his chairs, spinning around and around, alone in his shop.

A cop gets out of the car, shaking his fist at the radiator, then he fires a couple of shots at us, but we're too far away.

I fire a quick burst at one of the cars pursuing us, knocking out the glass in our rear window, then I lean out the side - window, firing at a cop car heading toward us, its lights flashing.

Billie hits the brakes, swerving onto the sidewalk.

Someone carrying a saxophone case is illuminated by our headlights, frozen there, like a deer in a spotlight, then we're past him, in the street again.

"Whew," Billie says.

I can't see the cop car now, but I can still hear its siren. I heard a woman screaming like that in the back room of an abortion mill.

I've never liked sirens at night.

By the time we hit Lake Shore Drive, we're doing eighty-five.

Snow and ice blow in through the open space where the rear window used to be, and the car's filled with shattered glass.

Billie's hair is blowing in the wind, and she's laughing.

"John, you've got to do something about that heater. It's freezing in here."

I'm comin' out of this after-hours club where I'm supposed to play later that night when this car races up onto the sidewalk. I hear guns firin' and sirens goin' and I hit the concrete fast, I can tell you. I'm lyin' there with my face in the snow, clutchin' my sax case.

Later, some cops come by, asking what I saw, and I tell them I didn't see nothin', it was all a blur.

They say, "That was John Dillinger."

I go back into the club and tell Tatum about it. He and I had played with Beiderbecke and we'd both backed up Lil Armstrong. She used to sing "Days Are Lonesome, Nights Are So Long," and, man, it was beautiful. Sometimes the three of us hung out together, juicin', smokin' a little dope.

Art was playin' intermission piano at the club, but he was on break. When I played with him before, I always used to bring a book with me 'cause he couldn't see. I used to read to him, while he'd sit there and drink beer. Man, I'd read and read and he'd drink and drink. I guess it didn't hurt him none since he didn't have to see what he was doin'.

I tell Art what happened out on the street, how the cops had been chasin' Dillinger and how I ended up with my face in the snow.

Art says, "You gotta read me a story about him, Tommy. Read me a story about Dillinger."

"You've been after me to take you out, so . . . here we are." I smile. "How do you like it?"

Mary sips an old-fashioned and looks around the place. The ceiling's twelve feet high, constructed of lath boards with a coat of white primer on them, and there must be more than a hundred dollar bills stuck to the ceiling.

I don't know how they got there.

"Johnnie takes Billie to the best nightspots in Chicago, and you bring me . . . here. To Volpi's. What kind of a place has a name like that?"

Mary makes it sound like a dirty word.

I take a sip of whiskey, chasing it with beer. I always liked coming here. It's quiet, and the deli out front makes some of the best sandwiches in Chicago. "It's the owner's name. Volpi. What do you think he should call it, the Ritz?"

"Yeah, it's ritzy all right. I haven't been to a place this ritzy since I went to the Hamburger Haven in Kansas City. All the time I was there, I kept thinking, No wonder Dorothy went to Oz."

Mary points toward a large glass case with a stuffed bird in it, and to a poster of a group of women with the title THE WEST'S MOST WANTED underneath the photo.

"What kind of a place has a picture with a bunch of prostitutes from the Old West hanging on the wall?" Mary asks.

"Don't look at it if it bothers you. Look at something else."

"Like what?"

"Like all the deer heads." There must be a dozen of them on the walls. "Or like that guy at the bar. Look at him. He's wearing workman's gloves and drinking beer."

"So what? Maybe there's something wrong with his hands."

I always thought Volpi's was one of the nicest speakeasies in Chicago, but it's hard to make some people happy. Especially women.

"Why do you think they call these places *speakeasies?*" I ask.

"How should I know?"

"You read all those books, that's why."

"Yeah, well, I never read anything about places like this."

I order more drinks and tell the bartender, "Just keep them coming," and give him a ten spot. He can keep the change.

Mary leans against the wall, her face softening as she sips her second old-fashioned. There's nothing like a few drinks at the end of a day. People let their guard down. Trust each other.

Mary says, "I read Prohibition might end next month."

"We've been hearin' that for thirteen years, but I'll drink to it."

"You'll drink to anything," Mary says, but she's smiling. We touch glasses.

"Everyone but Capone and some temperance ladies would be glad to see it go."

"And your friend, Mr. Volpi. Don't forget about him. He'd have to find a new line of work."

"Sometimes I think I ought to find a new line of work."

"Maybe you should," Mary says, touching my hand.

What the world needs is more trust.

"John and Billie could have been killed the other night, and the cops arrested Hank yesterday. He and some woman he picked up got into a fight. They were in his car, parked on the corner of North and Harlem, yelling at each other. I don't know what it was all about, but Hank pulled a revolver and began waving it at her."

"I never liked Hank," Mary says. "He was never a right guy. Never reliable. I could never figure out what Johnnie saw in him."

"They started out together, knocking over that bank in Daleville. It's a loyalty thing."

"I'm just glad Johnnie didn't get caught. I'm even glad Billie got away. I just wish she'd make breakfast once in awhile."

"Well, you can't have everything," I say.

PENNY HANCOCK

"It's Buffalo Nickel Day," the reporter says. "They're showing *To the Last Man* with Randolph Scott and Shirley Temple, and *Sagebrush Trail* with John Wayne at the Dream Theatre. Two movies for a nickel, and you can get a box of popcorn with melted butter for an extra five cents. I thought maybe you'd like to go."

I can tell he's a big spender. I invited him into the kitchen because it's snowing outside. Mom and I made sugar cookies shaped like candy canes this morning, so the kitchen's warm. The reporter and I sit across from one another at the wooden table.

"I don't know. I saw this Western with Tom Keene last month. He comes home from the World War and discovers one of his best friends was murdered and another was accused of the crime. The bad guys are from Chicago, of course, and they all have submachine guns, but they're no match for Keene's blazing pistols.

"I told Uncle Johnnie it was a stupid movie."

"So . . ." The reporter dips a candy cane into his coffee. "Will you go with me?"

"I'll have to think about it."

I can see the snow falling in great soft flakes through the kitchen window. Uncle Johnnie and I built a huge snowman one winter. When we'd finished, Johnnie placed two pieces of coal where the eyes should be and shouted, "I can see, I can see!" laughing in his delight.

"Uncle Johnnie says some of the bank robberies are pre-arranged affairs."

"I don't get it," the reporter says.

He told me his name's Lemon Moate, and he has brothers named Orange and Lime. His parents own an orchard in Pennsylvania, and they would have named a girl Cherry. It must be tough to go through life with a name like Lemon, but I'm still not sure I want to go to the movies with him.

"Bank presidents stage a robbery when they can't explain some of their losses. They've embezzled money, but they can cover their losses by falsifying the books and saying Uncle Johnnie got away with the money. They're the real crooks, stealing from their depositors. It's a setup. Uncle Johnnie may get five thousand dollars, but they'll claim he got away with twice that much, and no one gets hurt. Everyone acts out his part, like a movie."

"I can't publish a story like that," Lemon says. "They'd laugh me off the paper for saying a bank president robbed his own bank, and we'd be sued for libel."

"What kind of a reporter are you, anyway? I thought you were supposed to go after the truth."

"Only when it's believable."

"That's the dumbest thing I ever heard," I say. "I'm not going to the movies with someone named after a fruit."

HARRY PIERPONT

Some ladies from the American Legion Auxiliary League are bowling in the basement below the Hotel Racine. The alley's warm and brightly lit and it gives you a safe feeling, like home, although Mary and I almost have to shout at one another over the sound of the balls rolling down the lanes and the pins breaking. I kept score for one of the teams while I was waiting for Mary to come down from our room.

One of the ladies asked what I did for a living, and I told her I was a bank examiner. She thought it must be an exciting life, traveling from town to town, but I told her one hotel room looks like another after awhile. They all have a picture of some Indian maid in a canoe and there's always a Gideon Bible, but I told her I prefer to read the evening news. "I guess I'm just a heathen," I said, but she was sure that wasn't true.

I tell Mary, "Knocking over a bank on Monday always makes me feel like a good citizen, like I'm starting the week the way everyone else does—going to work."

"Some work," Mary says, watching a lady in lane 5 roll a gutter ball.

"It makes me feel like I'm one of those people who help keep America going."

"Yeah, pretty soon they'll make you an honorary member of the Eagles for your civic-mindedness."

"I had a cousin who was an Eagle. He could get a drink seven days a week, and they had a potluck every Sunday afternoon. He said the room always smelled of kielbassi and sauerkraut, and they had German beer on tap. To become a member, all he had to do was swear he loved God and his country and that he didn't have any nigger blood, but they could see that. He was a big blond guy with blue eyes."

"It sounds like a pretty good deal," Mary says.

"Yeah, someday I'm going to go back there."

I walk into the American Bank and Trust Company at 2:55 with a rolled-up Red Cross poster under my arm. The poster shows a young woman giving a soldier a pack of smokes as he heads overseas. It's captioned THEY BROUGHT OUR BOYS HOME.

I smile at one of the tellers, than I tape the poster into the left front window so no one will be able to see the tellers' cages from the street. It's a good plan.

John always comes up with a good plan, but Mary and I spent several days casing the place. I asked her why banks are always made out of stone, because she knows stuff like that. She thought for a moment, then said, "I guess it's because bankers have such hard hearts."

Once the poster's in place, Makley, Red, and John follow me into the bank.

We're all wearing overcoats, but no one will think it's strange. Not today. It may be fifty-two degrees outside, but it's a cruel wind blowing in from the lake.

John bought a blue Buick with yellow wire wheels, "Special for this job," he said. I told him it would be safer if we stuck to a black car that wouldn't attract so much attention, but he said it's important to do things with style. "Sometimes you need to make a statement."

Mary nodded. "I like a man with élan."

"Yeah, élan," I said. "Never leave home without it."

John smiled, but I could tell he didn't know what Mary was talking about, either. She might as well have been speaking Japanese.

Makley has two .45's and a submachine gun under his coat, so he almost clumps when he walks.

I told Mary he's the kind of guy who'd stick a gun up his ass if one would fit there, but what can you expect from someone who likes to watch a snake crawl up some dame's snatch?

Mary said, "I think he might be afraid it'd go off when he sat down. I know it'd worry me plenty."

Makley goes to one of the teller's windows and says, "Hands up," but the dumb sonofabitch doesn't even look up. I wonder if the bank makes him wear the elbow garter to stop him from slipping money up his sleeve. These bankers are cagey.

"Go to the next window, please."

"I don't feel like going to the next window," Makley says. "Don't you have any manners?" Then he shoots the teller through the right elbow.

That's when the alarm goes off.

JOHN DILLINGER

Red and I are in the vault when we hear the shot, then an alarm sounds. We keep stuffing fifties and hundreds into the canvas mailbags he stole from a post office in Chicago, but we move faster.

Red says, "I never liked the post office. I remember waitin' for the mail everyday when I was four or five. The mailman'd come by twice a day and he never brought me nothin'."

"What did you expect to get? You were a kid."

"I'd swear at him. You bastard. Fuckhead. I didn't even know what the words meant, but I heard my old man say them all the time. He always referred to his boss as a fuckhead, and I knew it couldn't be very nice. My old man couldn't say a sentence without usin' a dirty word when he was drunk, and he was drunk all the time."

I can barely hear him over the alarm, but the bags are almost full now. We'll be out of here in minutes.

"Mornin' and afternoon, mornin' and afternoon, the fuckin' postman would go by in his blue suit. He wouldn't even wave at me."

"Hurry up in there!" Makley yells. "There's a crowd gatherin' outside. You'd think they never saw a bank robbery before. They're all standin' there gawkin'."

"Maybe that's why I hate cops so much," Red says. "They remind me of mailmen."

There must be a hundred people milling around in front of the bank, gawking, when we get to the front door. The alarm's still jangling. It reminds me of the one that used to go off next to my bed every morning when I was a kid.

It was still there, ticking and jangling, when I got out of Michigan City, and it still got on my nerves. I blew it to pieces with my .45 while Dad stood there watching.

"Time flies," I said.

Makley cradles his Thompson, smiling, and Harry clutches the submachine gun he took from a cop who came barging in when he heard the alarm. Now the cop's lying facedown on the floor with a bloody head.

We nudge our hostages down the stone steps ahead of us, taking one step at a time. Slowly.

Mrs. Patzke's wearing a thin red dress, and she has her hands up. She keeps saying, "Don't shoot, don't shoot." Her dress flutters in the wind.

Mr. Weyland's wearing a pinstriped suit, and his bald head glistens in the feeble sunlight. I say, "You know, you could be a bank president. You've got that dignified look," but Weyland doesn't laugh.

As we push our way through the crowd Harry says, "Excuse me, excuse me, please." I almost expect him to pass out business cards, and tell people he's running for office. Maybe he'd stop and kiss a baby if one were handy.

Two cops get out of a squad car at the edge of the crowd, moving toward us carefully, but Makley fires a burst from his Thompson, breaking the windows in the Wylie Hat shop.

Everyone begins to scream, falling to the street, running, bumping into each other, the glass shattering. Makley fires another burst, knocking out the letter *S* in *Bombshell* on the marquee at the Venetian Theatre.

I tell Weyland, "I want to see that movie, *Bombhell*, with Jean Harlow. It's supposed to be a good one," but he still doesn't laugh. Someone ought to buy him a sense of humor.

We break away from the crowd, turning the corner into the bank parking lot. There's a sign saying FOR CUSTOMERS ONLY. ALL OTHERS WILL BE TOWED AWAY.

Makley nudges Weyland with the Thompson and says, "How come you're not friendlier, huh?" but Weyland doesn't answer, even when Makley jabs him harder. "Huh, huh?"

I get behind the wheel of the Buick and Makley sits across from me. Harry and Red are in back, and Mrs. Patzke and Weyland stand on the running boards. The cops won't get too close as long as we've got hostages.

Weyland says, "I want you men to know I'm not forgetting this. None of it. I never forget a face."

Makley twists Weyland's wrist and says, "We don't like bank presidents. We'd as soon shoot you as look at you, so I'd shut up if I were you."

"He's just kidding," Harry says, lighting a Camel with a wooden match he strikes with his thumbnail. I can smell sulfur when he blows it out.

Makley says, "The hell I am," as I drive out of town. "Some prick had my car towed away from a bank parking lot, and I ain't forgetting it."

"Sometimes I think I should have stayed in California," Red says. "I was just a kid when I was out there. I didn't know nothin'."

"You was never a kid," Makley says.

"It was before my hair went gray around the edges." He seems wistful.

"You're still Red to us," I say.

We pass a funeral procession leaving a small cemetery. There's a stone fence around it, and a wrought-iron gate over the road leading in. They buried my mother on a day like this. I was only three, but I remember.

"I worked with this gang of whiskey runners. We brought the hooch into Tomales Bay on fishin' boats and stored it in these milk cans that must have held fifty gallons. We unloaded the hooch at this cove near a little place called Marshall. They had all these trees that's been brought in from Australia. A guy I worked with thought they smelled like a cat in heat, but they didn't smell like any cat I was ever around."

I wave at a farmer coming toward us on a wagon filled with hay, and he waves back, smiling. The wagon's being drawn by two spotted horses, and the farmer's face is red from the wind.

My mother's face was pale.

"There were all these wop dairy farmers along the bay, so everything looked kosher. Everyone thought we were haulin' milk."

"You now where they got the word *wop?*" Makley asks.

"What kind of a question is that? Who cares?"

"*Wop*'s the sound spaghetti makes when it hits the ceiling."

Mrs. Patzke laughs. She's sitting on Red's lap, and Weyland's scrunched in between them and Harry. He looks as comfortable as some guy at an opera.

"That's the dumbest thing I ever heard," Red says. "Why would someone throw spaghetti on the ceiling?"

"So they'll know if it's done or not. It sticks to the ceiling when it's done."

"I can see some wops throwin' plates of spaghetti on the ceilin'. It would make a hell of a mess. Who cleans up after 'em?"

"Never mind," Makley says. "I'm sorry I mentioned it."

"Most of the guys I worked with were wops," Red says. "They all stuck together. It was a funny thing. I saw them knock guys off on

Saturday night, but the next mornin' they'd be on their fuckin' knees at this Catholic church in Tomales. Most of the ceremony was in Latin, so I know they didn't understand a fuckin' word the priest said. Then they'd go up to the altar and stick their tongues out, like they had a sore throat or somethin', and the priest would give 'em a cough drop."

"It's a wafer," Makley says. "A wafer."

"It looked like a cough drop to me, but what do I know? I never understood how come the priest dressed like a drag queen. It was pretty fuckin' weird."

Harry says, "Cut it out, Red. You don't need to swear so much. Remember, we've got a lady in here."

"How can I forget? She's on my lap; I've had a hard-on for the last hour."

The wind's colder now. There's a grove of sugar maples in the distance, and you can see a farmhouse with a sagging green roof at the end of the road.

Sometimes I think they'll gun me down in a place like this, burying me beneath the sugar maples. They'd mark my grave with a cross made out of twigs and scratch my name, Dillinger, on a small stone. I wonder if anyone would mourn me.

Harry and Mary hid cans of gas in the trees, so we can re-fuel without stopping at a service station.

I pull over next to the sugar-maple grove, filling the car with gas, while Harry points to the farmhouse. "You should be able to get a ride there." He loaned Mrs. Patzke his camel's-hair coat when she was shivering. He says, "I'm sorry, but I'll need it back now. You don't have far to go." He almost seems embarrassed.

"I appreciate your kindness," Mrs. Patzke says, then she and Weyland head toward the farmhouse.

Makley watches me pouring gas and says, "You could probably get a job at that Mobil station we passed. They'd probably give you a pair of overalls with one of those flying horses stitched on the pocket. It'd be whole new career."

"It might not be a bad idea." I say.

DON STEELE

"You want to know about the robbery. I'll tell you about the robbery. The teller next to me was lyin' on the floor with blood leakin' out of what used to be his elbow. I asked Harold if I could do anything, then I ran down the street to a place that was padlocked and in the back door.

"I paid three dollars for a pint and went back to the bank, where I poured a pretty good Dixie cupfull. I asked Harold if he wanted it and he refused, so three or four of us killed the bottle. Then we balanced the books.

"I went out and had a few more drinks and some oysters and walked home sober as a judge, I swear to God. I didn't begin to feel the effects until two or three days after the holdup. Then I trembled so I could hardly stand up. I'll tell you this, mister. When you look down the barrel of a forty-five it looks like a cannon."

BILLIE FRECHETTE

"I'm sorry we have to move again," John says, looking toward Lake Michigan. Clouds rush across a mother-of-pearl sky, and we can see the waves breaking on the beach. "I'll miss the view."

"I'll even miss Mary's Polack stories," I say.

Two suitcases are on the bed, and there's a large box filled with guns and ammunition. You have to keep moving when you're in this business. It's a month here, a month there. Sometimes you get lucky and you can stay sixty days, maybe even ninety.

We can hear people partying on the floor below us. Prohibition was repealed by the Twenty-first Amendment, and there's a bar across town by that name.

I say, "We can get a drink and it will be legal."

"Yeah, but it won't be as much fun," John says.

We sip our drinks, watching the crowd at the bar. It seems strange to be sitting here. We didn't have to give someone a password at the door, and there are gilt letters on the window: THE TWENTY-FIRST AMENDMENT.

"I guess my only bad habit is robbing banks," John says. "I don't smoke much, and I drink even less."

"Robbing banks isn't such a bad habit," I say. "Someone has to do it, and you're good at it."

Roosevelt claimed he'd get rid of Prohibition if we voted him in as president. At last—a politician who kept his word.

John's glass rings when it touches mine. I like the sound of good crystal. "To Roosevelt."

"To Roosevelt. I just wish his fireside chats weren't so dull."

I ordered a dry martini and John ordered a Gibson, but they taste the same to me.

"What's the difference?" I ask.

"Yours comes with a green olive and mine comes with a pearl onion."

"That's it?"

"Yeah."

"Why'd you order the one with the onion?"

"I never liked green things," he says.

"You never told me why everyone calls you 'Billie' instead of 'Evelyn.'"

"I don't know. I guess kids started to call me that when I was on the reservation, and it just stuck."

"I thought your father might have wanted a boy, and he'd decided on the name Billy. Then you came along, and he was too lazy to change his mind."

"He was lazy, all right, but I don't think he'd decided on a name."

John frowns, watching me eat the olive, sucking the gin from it. My lips pucker.

People at the bar toast each other, hugging. I've watched strangers kiss on impulse, watched them laugh and cry.

An elderly lady at the end of the bar is weeping, and the old gentleman with her says, "We do well not to grieve on and on," his hand on her shoulder.

I hope John will touch me like that years from now. I say, "The reservation kids thought I was a tomboy. My breasts were small and I could never afford makeup."

"It's hard to imagine."

"A lot of things are, John. If someone had told me I'd be sitting across from you six months ago, I'd have laughed."

"I hope you're not sorry."

"I wouldn't have it any other way."

WINTER 1933–1934

It's begun to snow when we go into a small tavern at the edge of Mooresville. The red sun sinks into the furrowed earth outside, turning the land lavender just before the coming of complete night. The sky gradually fades to the color of bitterroot along the horizon.

Billie and I sit at the bar because it's cozy. I order a Schlitz and she orders Chablis, and we watch the softly falling snow through the tavern window while the bartender brings us our drinks.

"It's too bad about Red," Billie says. "He must have been in a tight spot, killing that cop in Chicago."

Officer Shanley had confronted Red and his girlfriend in a parking garage, and there'd been a shoot-out when Red couldn't produce the registration to the car he was driving. Red escaped, leaving the girl there. She was holding the mink coat he'd given her when the cops came and she told them, "I don't care what anyone says. He was awfully nice."

I tell Billie, "Red's the only guy I know who didn't get into trouble when he was in Michigan City. I think it had something to do with his sister. She was head of the PTA, and she was always sending him these pamphlets about virtue being its own reward. That kind of stuff. The screws only came down on him once, and that was for skipping rope."

"Why would they punish someone for skipping rope?"

"They don't want you to have any fun," I say. "That's the way screws are."

BILLIE FRECHETTE

John and I walk by the Idle Hour Theatre and he tells me, "I idled away a lot of hours there when we moved to Mooresville. I must have seen every film that came to town, most of them two or three times."

We stand in front of the Idle Hour in the softly falling snow, and John gestures theatrically. He's dyed his hair red and grown a mustache to hide a small scar on his lip. He could be Red's brother.

"When I wasn't at the movies, I was at Gaffey's Poolroom, across the street. It didn't matter if I had any money or not. Gaffey always let me play. He was that kind of guy. I wish there were more like him."

We walk along, hands in our coat pockets, admiring the brightly-lit Christmas trees and the display windows filled with wreathes and garland. We could be a pair of young lovers on our way to a party, but John has a .38 in the shoulder holster under his coat.

"It's kind of funny," he says.

"What is?"

"I couldn't wait to get out of this town when I was a kid, but I keep coming back."

"I'm never going back to the reservation," I say. "I don't even want to drive past it."

JOHN DILLINGER

A woman in her mid-thirties is standing in front of the tavern when we go back to our car. She has two kids with her, and she's holding a sign that says EVERYBODY NEEDS HELP SOMETIME. WILL

WORK FOR FOOD OR LODGING. She has dirty-blond hair and large eyes that make her look frightened.

I'd be frightened, too.

Down the street, some carollers are singing, "Silent Night, Holy Night."

The woman and kids are wearing thin coats, wet from the falling snow, and their faces are red and blue from the lights in the window of the tavern. Red and blue. They stand there shivering. Oh little town . . . of Mooresville.

Someone I met in the joint told me, "We were so poor we learned to eat stones." He and his wife and kids lived in a Hooverville near the railroad tracks outside Indianapolis. They picked up chunks of coal that fell off the trains, and he said winter was always the worst time of year.

Now the carollers are singing "Jingle Bells."

Later, they'll go back to their warm homes, their faces flushed, and drink hot toddies and listen to the radio.

"Merry Christmas," I say, handing the woman a hundred-dollar bill, then Billie and I get into our car.

The woman stands there holding the bill, looking at it in the red-and-blue light while the snow comes down, then she runs toward our car. She says "God bless you" over and over, her breath steaming in the freezing air.

I smile and wave, then pull away from the curb. I watch her, frozen there, in the rearview mirror, then she's lost in the falling snow.

I take the road out of town toward Dad's farm, quiet for a long time, listening to the windshield wipers clack. Billie and I will be in Florida in four days.

We'll meet the gang there.

"People shouldn't have to eat stones."

"Huh?" Billie says.

AUDREY HANCOCK

Johnnie and Billie take their coats off, smiling, when they come into the parlor. I give Johnnie a Schlitz, his favorite, and Billie has some warm eggnog with rum. My husband and daughter bring the drinks out from the kitchen, then they hang tinsel and popcorn balls on the tree we cut from the back field earlier today. It must be nine feet tall.

We could almost pass for an ordinary family, but I know Johnnie will be gone before it's daylight. Johnnie is always going, and I always give him a big hug before he leaves.

I never know if I'll see him alive again.

I tell Billie, "I was seventeen when Mom died. Johnnie was only three, so I was more of a mother to him than a sister."

"Pretty soon she'll drag out my baby pictures," Johnnie says. He crosses his legs and smiles. "You know, the kind that always embarrass you when you're older." He looks funny with red hair.

"There's an adorable one of Johnnie in a washtub when he was just a few months old. The only thing he's wearing is his smile," I say.

"What the hell would she want to look at that for?" Dad asks. He's standing on a ladder, putting an angel on top of the tree. "One naked baby looks like another."

"Not if you have the right eyes," I tell him.

"My eyes are fine," he says. "I've only worn these damn glasses for the last couple of years. I see things, all right."

"He was so chubby he looked like he had the mumps," I say.

Later, we'll go into the kitchen and eat a late supper. I knew Johnnie was coming so I made fried chicken and frog legs, and there's coconut-cream pie, his favorite, because Johnnie always gets what Johnnie wants.

I remember he used to beg me to take him to the movies on Saturday afternoon. I liked to pretend I was too busy, that I had to wash clothes and hang them on the line out back, and there were the chickens to feed.

"Aw, come on, Sis, you've got to take me," he'd say. "This one's special. It's called *The Squaw Man* and it's got cowboys and Indians and everything." Johnnie must have been eleven when we saw that.

Sometimes he'd sneak off to the movies by himself, but Dad and I always knew where to find him.

Maybe we should have punished Johnnie. I don't know. Maybe he grew up believing he could get away with anything. That no matter what he did, people would love him for it. In a way, he was right. A lot of people in town cheer every time he robs a bank.

When Dad comes down from the ladder, the six of us go into the kitchen. Before we eat I say, "Dear Father, bless this food and bless these people at our table."

I don't want to take any chances while Johnnie's here.

Dad eats a drumstick, his false teeth clacking, and says, "I still say one naked baby looks like another."

JOHN DILLINGER

Billie and I go out onto the back porch after dinner. It's still snowing, the flakes swirling in the yellow light from the kitchen. I tell her, "It was snowing the day I got out of the navy."

"I didn't know you were in the navy."

"Yeah, for a while. I was a fireman third class, but I got tired of people telling me what to do."

"How come I'm not surprised?" Billie asks.

"They gave me ten days in solitary for being absent without leave. And when I went AWOL again, they added another five days. I told them I was never very good at telling time—I got an *F* in arithmetic—and walked off the boat one night. We were in Boston harbor." I light a cigarette, watching the tip of it glow when I inhale. "They kept telling me it was a ship, not a boat, but I could never make the distinction. Boat, ship, who the hell cared? It was named the USS *Utah*, probably because life on board was as exciting as it is in Utah. I don't know how many days I would have gotten for being AWOL that time, because I never went back."

Billie's silhouetted against the light coming through the kitchen window.

"Didn't they come looking for you?"

"No. They listed me as a deserter and put a fifty-dollar price on my head. It seemed like a lot then but, hell, I was just getting started. Now it's up to fifteen thousand, and they want to kill me."

"What did you tell people when you came home?"

"About what?"

"About getting out early."

"I told them I failed arithmetic. I could never figure out the difference between latitude and longitude."

"What *is* the difference?"

"Damned if I know."

Billie laughs, then we go back into the house filled with friendly voices and laughter and the smell of good things.

RED HAMILTON

Makley looks out at the ocean, sipping a gin and tonic, from the porch of the house Billie rented in Daytona. It has seventeen rooms and a private beach, and there's room for everyone. I would have thought the place was a palace when I was growing up.

"I didn't mind shootin' that cop so much; he should have minded his own business, but I hated to leave Elaine behind," I say. "She was somethin' special."

"They're all special," Makley says.

"I mean it. She was a classy dame."

"A waitress with class, huh?"

"What's wrong with waitresses?"

"Nothin', I guess. But *class* isn't the first word that comes to mind when I think of them. I picked one up at this joint in Atlanta. She had these incredible knockers. You'd think you were Sharkey goin' down in the sixth round against Carnera if she hit you on the head with 'em. The Cut Throat Saloon, that was the name of the joint."

"Talk about classy-sounding places," I say.

"There were these brassieres all over the ceilin'. There must have been a hundred of them. All shapes and sizes. It was the damndest thing you ever saw. I asked the bartender why they were hangin' there, and he told me anyone who took her bra off and gave the customers a free look got a T-shirt with the name of the joint on it."

"There must not be much to do in Atlanta."

"This waitress was sitting at the bar drinkin' when she decides it's too hot or somethin' and takes off her bra. I fell in love with her instantly."

"She didn't happen to have a snake, did she?"

JOHN DILLINGER

"Who the fuck was Ponce de León?" Red asks.

"He came here from Spain more than four hundred years

ago," I say. "He believed he and his men would live forever if they could find the Fountain of Youth."

We've seen Ponce de León gift shops and restaurants, and there's a life-sized statue of a conquistador in the park on the Avenida Ponce de León. It's rusting away from the salt air, so even a statue doesn't "live forever," but that doesn't stop the merchants from cashing in on his name. They're selling "curative" waters bottled at Ponce de León Springs.

"Why would anyone want to live forever?" Red asks.

"I don't think it's something we have to worry about," I say.

"I think my old man wanted to live forever," Red says, "but he died when I was seven. He was a goofy fuck. I remember one Thanksgiving, he went out into the backyard with a shovel and dug this big hole. I'm maybe five at the time and I'm standin' there watchin' him. It's cold in the Upper Peninsula in November, the ground's frozen, so he has to dig like a sonofabitch. I could see the sweat stains under his arms. I keep askin' him, 'What're you gonna bury, huh?' and he finally stops, leanin' on his shovel, and says, 'You really want to know?' and I nod, and he tells me, 'Your little brother,' then he throws the carcass of the turkey into the hole. It's beginnin' to snow and I'm standing there cryin'. I yell, 'I don't have no little brother!' then I run into the house. My sister said I didn't cry that much when my fingers was sliced off by the sled. I don't know what made my old man so mean—why would he say somethin' like that?—but, later, it made sense when he died from a bum heart."

MARY KINDER

Harry and I are sitting next to the swimming pool behind the house. I say, "I don't know why anyone would want a pool in back when there's all that ocean out front, but some writer said the rich are different than you and me."

"Yeah, they have more money." Harry laughs.

"Maybe the people who built the place were afraid of the ocean. I kept getting knocked over by the waves when I went wading."

"That's because you're so tiny."

"Someone told me there're sharks out there. They can take your leg off like that." I snap my fingers. "Maybe a pool isn't such a bad idea."

"Maybe not," Harry says. "Why don't you rub some suntan lotion on my back?"

JOHN DILLINGER

I come up for air at the end of the pool, gasping, shaking the water from my face.

Billie's there.

She's wearing a one-piece blue bathing suit, her nipples protruding through the silk.

I can feel the ceramic tiles against my back as Billie laughs, delighted, her legs straddling me. I can feel her fingers groping at the edge of my suit beneath the water. She touches me . . . there. Oh, Billie.

I put my arms around her, feeling myself harden. I pull her suit aside and we move together, slowly, in the warm water. The sky stretches out to the sea.

We made love in a cabin once during the winter. There was a blue sky that day. I built a fire in the woodstove, naked, feeling the heat on the tip of my penis—it glowed—and Billie said, "Don't burn it."

Then we lay on a large rug, while the last of the leaves fell from the tree outside our window.

She was straddling me when we came one afternoon, and I remember scootching across the bed, Billie riding me, reaching for the towel she kept there. I wanted to yell *yippee.*

Billie claims it isn't so messy that way, sharing a towel, but I've never minded wet sheets.

She said, "I like the sound of the word, scootching."

I've never come underwater before.

It's a strange feeling, the pressure building until you think you'll never come, that it must be impossible underwater. Then you feel the release, and you watch the cum rising slowly, glistening in the sunlight, watch it surface.

Billie puts a drop of it onto her finger, then tastes it, saying, "It's salty, John, like those crackers the Japs eat that are made from kelp or seaweed or something."

"If you say so."

She holds her finger up to the sun, the cum glistening. "Look," she says, "it sparkles like a pearl."

BILLIE FRECHETTE

"Maybe we should move here, John. You can rob banks anywhere. That's one nice thing about your line of work. Mary says you and Harry are peripatetic."

"Yeah?"

"You move around a lot."

"That's us, all right. Peripatetic. Especially when the cops are after us." John laughs.

We're sitting on the floor, leaning against the couch, next to the tree. Outside, the moon hovers over the water. I like this time of night, neither morning nor evening. Mary says night furls in on itself. I don't know what she means, but it has a nice sound.

Everyone else has gone to bed, and John and I drink what's left of the champagne. He gave me a diamond ring for

Christmas, and I gave him a pen-and-pencil set. The diamond sparkles in the light from the fireplace. John talks about what it will be like when we're married someday. I think the ring's as close as we'll ever get, but maybe that's the Indian in me. Growing up on the reservation makes you fatalistic.

John says, "It's funny. I hate cold weather, but it doesn't seem like Christmas without snow."

"I'd like it fine if it were eighty degrees every day. My legs don't ache so much."

"Sis always took me sled riding after the first snow."

"I always got sick during the winter when I was a kid on the reservation. One Christmas I even got the measles. I woke up and there were these spots all over my face.

"I know people who get all gaga looking at the leaves change color in the autumn, but it just means things are dying, John. Seasons are overrated. It would be all right with me if I never saw snow again. I don't even want to see it on a damn calendar."

JOHN DILLINGER

We can hear the pig squealing over the sound of the outboard motor. The pig's being dragged by a twenty-foot rope, and we watch it gliding across the waves in the moonlight. It looks like it's waterskiing.

"I think this was a dumb idea," Makley says. "You should never plan anything when you're drunk." He's wearing a Panama hat he bought when we came to Daytona and a white suit made out of linen. He spends most of his time drinking gin and tonics. Before long, he'll have to hire some kid to fan him with a giant palm frond. Maybe he hopes some movie producer will cast him in a movie that takes place in the tropics, but he still looks like the Little King to me.

"How hard can it be to track down a fourteen-foot alligator named 'Old Joe'?" Red asks.

He and I are holding Thompsons, looking for some sign of Old Joe, while Makley steers the boat. We can see the lights from Daytona Beach on the horizon.

"It's obviously harder than we thought," Makley says. "I haven't seen anything but that pig out there. Old Joe should have come for him by now."

"Maybe Old Joe doesn't like pork," Red says. "Maybe he's a Moslem or somethin'."

"Alligators eat anything, for Christ sake. They eat tin cans."

"No, that's goats. Goats eat tin cans."

"What's the difference? Alligators, goats. Who the hell cares?"

The boat's rocking and the spray from the ocean flies up into our faces, and the sound the pig makes is terrible. I didn't know pigs could make so much noise.

"This is what happens when you try to perform a public service," Red says. "Old Joe's going to wipe out all the cats in Daytona Beach if we don't stop him."

"Yeah, it's good we're not in business as alligator exterminators. We'd go broke in a hurry."

"At least I'm going to have some fun before we go back to shore," Red says.

He fires the Thompson at the moon, the stars, the sea, spraying lead everywhere. He laughs.

Maybe the Chinese have the right idea, bringing in the new year with fireworks.

"Happy New Year," I say and begin firing my Thompson, but the screams of the pig almost drown out the bursts from our submachine guns.

"*The Three Little Pigs* was my favorite movie of the year," I say, "but I'm getting not to like pigs."

"Me neither," Red says.

He aims at the pig, firing a quick burst on the Thompson, and we watch the pig disappear beneath the waves. It looks like there's an oil slick on the water where the pig used to be.

"I got tired of listenin' to it," Red says.

HARRY PIERPONT

"People die out here," Mary says.

There're no trees or water, just an auto court and a diner with no name. People die everywhere. Some calico kittens forage for food next to our room, and the wind blows sand into our faces.

"I don't even know where the hell we are."

"Somewhere east of the Grand Canyon. Somewhere west of Oz."

When we go into the diner, a blond waitress in her forties hands us a flyspecked menu, and I can smell the grease from the grill.

I order a Pabst Blue Ribbon.

"We have iced tea or lemonade."

"I thought Prohibition was over."

"Not here," the blonde says. "This is a dry county." You can tell she's glad. The last boyfriend she had beat her when he got drunk, and she came here when it ended. Her face is eroded by the sun.

"So where do I get a beer?"

"Eighteen miles down the road—that way."

She looks bored, pointing south.

"Give me the iced tea," I say.

"I don't like it," Mary says. "I don't like anything about it."

"What are you, a fortune-teller?"

We lie on the double bed in our room, petting one of the kittens that followed us.

Mary says, "I don't need a crystal ball. It's just a feeling. We shouldn't be going to Tucson."

"Sure, we should. Makley knows this girl who sings in a club there."

"Makley knows a girl everywhere."

"He says Tucson's a wide-open town. You can have fun there. Party. It even has three houses of prostitution that operate in the open."

"That's a real incentive."

Mary feeds the kitten part of a leftover chicken sandwich, and the kitten works its claws into the bedspread, purring. It likes the chicken better than I did.

"Makley says there're still hitching posts on the main streets. It's like something out of the Old West. There's still room to breathe."

"I can breathe fine," Mary says. "Why did Johnnie go back to Chicago?"

"He wanted to pull one more job before he left. He gets bored if he goes too long without working. You know."

"That'll be the death of him someday."

"What will? Work?"

"Pulling one more job."

JOHN DILLINGER

"Elaine was a sensible woman," Red says.

He and I are sitting in the backseat of a blue Plymouth, and Makley's driving.

"That was something I liked about her. But one day she comes back from this shopping spree with a miniature cuckoo clock she bought at a thrift shop."

"The big spender," Makley says, glancing over his shoulder. "He sends his women to thrift shops."

"Maybe you should have given her more money," I say.

"I give her plenty. She just likes hangin' out at those dumps. She shows me this clock and says, 'Look what I got.' It has a couple of Christmas trees on this little platform and some toadstools with red-and-white dots and this deer standin' in what's supposed to be snow."

"I never heard of toadstools with red-and-white dots," Makley says. "Were they supposed to be poisonous?"

"How the hell should I know? What kind of a question is that?" Red asks.

He and I check our bulletproof vests, making sure they're fastened securely.

The streets are filled with slush.

"Elaine says the clock sold for two bucks, but she got it for fifty cents because the hour hand don't work. She's kind of proud of that, getting' it for four bits."

We drive by some buildings made of dirty red brick. Inside them are cafeterias and offices and people who hate their jobs.

"I asked Elaine, 'Why'd you buy a clock that don't work?' and she told me, 'I bought it because I like the way it looks. It's Christmasy.' That's what she said, 'Christmasy.' I don't think there is such a word."

"That's the dumbest thing I ever heard," Makley says, parking the Plymouth in front of the bank.

Red and I go up the stairs together. He's carrying a Federal Reserve sack, and I'm carrying the Thompson in a trombone case.

There's a skylight in the bank's ceiling, but the light's murky because it's a gray day. The faces of the people seem diffused.

I open the trombone case, pointing the machine gun at one of the cashiers and say, "This is a stickup! Put up your hands, everybody!" moving the Thompson in a slow arc, while Red goes behind the tellers' cages.

"What the fuck does someone do with a busted clock?" he says.

A customer points at some money he received for cashing a check and says, "Take it, but please don't hurt me;" then he raises his hands, standing on the tips of his toes, as if that will help him reach higher.

I say, "We don't want your money, just the bank's," but he still stands there on his tiptoes.

They're firing at us as Red and I come down the bank steps. Red staggers, falling, when a slug penetrates his vest.

I help him into the front seat of the car as blood oozes out of the small hole. Red looks at it and says, "I thought the damn things were supposed to be bulletproof."

Makley loses the cops in less than a mile, taking the turns we've mapped out beforehand. He lights a cigarette and says, "I met this blonde who works as a singer at a club in Tucson. That's what made me think we ought to go there."

"I don't care about some dame who's a singer," Red says.

"I heard her sing 'Empty Bed Blues' one night and I told her, 'Baby, your bed doesn't have to be empty anymore.' I knew I was in love."

"You're always in love," Red says.

"Not like this." Makley corners sharply, blowing smoke. "I gave her a hundred bucks and asked if she'd sing it again. May wondered what I did to earn a living and I told her I sold plumbing supplies. She said, 'You're lucky I'm blond because I believe you, but don't ever tell that story to a woman with dark hair.'"

"Fuck the blonde," Red says. "You're gotta get me to a doctor."

ELIZABETH O'MARA

"At the time John Dillinger was a student of mine he showed no inclination to steal. Other boys, you know, had stolen change from my desk. But John, although he had ample opportunity to do so, never touched a cent.

"He was intensely interested in anything mechanical, caring little for academic subjects. His grades were bad, so sometimes he would sign his own report card or tell his father he'd lost it, but all boys are like that. They tear up their lessons or lose them and are always thinking up some prank. Johnnie was mischievous like the rest of them, but he was such a healthy normal specimen of boy that you couldn't help liking him. I'll never forget one thing about him: He always tipped his hat to me."

HARRY PIERPONT

May Miller's breasts are almost falling out of the low-cut gown she's wearing. She leans toward the audience, hanging onto the microphone as if it's the only thing that's keeping her from swooning. Her platinum hair shines in the spotlight as she finishes "I'm Wild About That Thing."

I'll bet she is.

I whisper to Mary, "I think her hair came out of a bottle."

Makley's sitting across from us, his mouth open, watching May intently. He's still wearing the Panama hat he bought in Florida, and it looks weird out west. I keep telling him he ought to buy a Stetson.

"Maybe two bottles," Mary says. "She makes Jean Harlow look like a brunette."

"Those other dames who warble in clubs around town are singers," Makley says, "but May, she's a chanteuse." He seems breathless, like someone with asthma.

113

"What's the difference?" I ask.

"Class," Makley says. "A chanteuse is what they call those dames who sing in basement cabarets in Paris. It's Frenchified."

May nods at Mary and shakes hands with me when she joins us at our booth. She says, "Real pleased to meet 'cha," then she leans against Makley, as if she's still ready to swoon, and he puts an arm around her.

"Isn't she a babe?" Makley asks.

BILLIE FRENCHETTE

"We've got to get the little guy some dog chow," I say.

John bought me a Boston bull puppy we saw in the window of a pet store in Oklahoma City. I put my nose to the window and the pup leaped up, licking the glass.

"Look, it wants to kiss me," I said.

"You can't fault its taste."

"You've got to buy him for me, John."

"Why don't I buy you a diamond necklace instead? That way we won't have to stop every fifty miles so someone can walk the dog. I had a cocker spaniel when I was a kid in Indianapolis. The mailman got mad because Shep bit him."

"We're never anyplace long enough to get mail."

"Okay," John said, "if you promise to walk the dog."

John and Copper come back from the park down the street while I'm fixing dinner.

John told me he wanted to call the dog "Copper" so he'd remember to stay away from him. "I guess it didn't work," John says, shrugging.

"Did you have a nice walk?"

"Yeah, it was great. Everyone wanted to pet Copper, especially the young women. They all wanted to know what breed he is."

John opens a bottle of Schlitz, and the pork chops sizzle when I turn them over in the frying pan. I'll pour some of the grease onto the potatoes, along with some strips of bacon and green onions. I never thought I'd like cooking. I even made my own Roquefort dressing for the salad.

John smiles. "There're some beautiful women in this town."

"Maybe a dog wasn't such a great idea," I say.

CHARLES MAKLEY

"Red and I kid each other a lot, but I wish he was here. It doesn't feel right with him back in Illinois somewhere."

I park the Studebaker in front of Grabe's Electric and Radio, and May opens her compact.

"You're just jumpy," she says, studying her face in the mirror. "You need to relax, have more fun. You're even workin' when you're in bed, like some guy who read a manual on how to do it and wants to make sure every move is right." May dabs some powder onto her nose, nodding. "It isn't life and death." Satisfied, she puts the compact back into her purse. "Getting shot, like Red, that's life and death."

"Red'll be fine."

"That's what I've been tellin' you," May says.

Grabe's has a musty smell when we go inside, as if someone saved newspapers that had been left out in the rain, but it never rains here. An old guy standing behind the counter squints at us, one eye askew, and I want to ask if there's something wrong.

I say, "I'd like to look at one of those radios that picks up police calls."

"You won't be needing a radio," someone says, coming up behind me. "You're under arrest."

I turn around slowly.

A wiry cop with thinning blond hair sticks a pistol into my ribs, patting me down, while three other cops stand in the doorway. It looks like a cop convention.

"My name's J.C. Davies, from Jacksonville, Florida," I say. "I owned an auto-repair shop there but sold it. My doctor told me the dry air here would be good for my allergies. You must have made some mistake."

"You're the one who made a mistake," the cop says. "You shouldn't have thrown all that jack around on wine, women, and song. Someone recognized you from a photo in *True Detective Story*. That's the trouble with you guys. You all think you're lover boys."

MARY KINDER

"Someone's standing on the sidewalk out front."

I motion for Harry to come to the window.

"It's a Western Union boy," Harry says. "Look at the cap he's wearing."

"Why's he standing there, looking at our house?"

"How should I know? Maybe he's lost."

"I never heard of a Western Union boy getting lost," I say.

The "boy" must be thirty. He looks at the envelope he's holding, then he comes up the walkway to our porch, ringing the bell.

"What'll I do?"

"Answer the door," Harry says, standing to one side so the messenger won't see him.

"What do you want?" I ask, opening the door.

"I have a message for Mr. Thompson from Mr. Davies," the messenger says.

Thompson's the name we've been using in Tucson.

"I'll take it."

"I'm sorry, Mr. Thompson has to sign for it."

"I'm Mrs. Thompson."

"Mr. Thompson has to accept it personally. It's the rules."

The messenger puts his left foot over the threshold, holding the envelope and a pencil. The screen door flaps against his back in the late afternoon breeze.

"Okay, I'll take it," Harry says.

"You're Mr. Thompson?"

"Yeah."

"You're under arrest then."

"The hell I am," Harry says.

Then the two of them are struggling for a pistol the cop's pulled as I slam the door on the finger of someone who's come running onto the porch. I can hear him yelling, "I think she broke it, it's broken!" I lock the door and Harry smashes the cop in the face with his right hand, groping for the pistol with his left, I pummel the cop with my fists, hitting him on the back of his head, screaming, "Let go of Harry, you bastard!" while someone's hammering at the door and people are yelling, "Don't let 'em get away," the door collapses, splintering, and there're people pulling at me, hitting, the cop's nose is bleeding and there's blood on Harry's fist, "Break it up, break it up," there must be half a dozen cops in the room, one of them brings the butt of his pistol down on Harry's head, then the cop brings it down again and again I yell, "Don't hurt him, I can't stand it, please don't hit him anymore!"

JOHN DILLINGER

"I never saw a river with cactus growing in it before," Billie says.

There's sand where the water ought to be when we cross the bridge spanning the riverbed, and the wind's rising.

We take Copper for a walk in the park, and he barks at a statue of a forgotten doughboy, his metallic eyes glinting in the late afternoon light. Dust devils swirl around him as he stands there forlornly, holding his rifle.

A tarnished plaque at the foot of the statue claims: THOSE WHO GAVE THEIR LIVES FOR FREEDOM DID NOT DIE IN VAIN, then it lists the names of the dead from Pima County.

Copper sniffs at the plaque, then raises a leg, pissing on the statue.

It's dark when we pull up in front of the house we rented, but the lights in the neighbor's cottage are on, and I can hear the radio playing.

We walk past the chinaberry tree onto our porch, and Copper follows us, his nails scratching on the wood. The moon's large.

As I'm opening the door, someone shouts, "Stick 'em up!"

Billie and I turn around, slowly, our hands raised.

Two cops are pointing their pistols at us and a third one's holding a sawed-off shotgun.

Copper barks at them, and one of the cops swears, "Get the goddamn mutt to shut up."

I say, "My name's John Donovan and this is my wife, Annie. We're from Wisconsin."

"Yeah, and I'm the emperor of Ethiopia," the cop with the shotgun says. "We know who you are. Dillinger." He makes it sound dirty.

The cop who swore frisks me, taking the .45 automatic from my shoulder holster. His breath stinks.

"Well, well, what do we have here?"

"I'm a businessman. I carry large sums of money, and I need to protect myself."

"Yeah, we know what business you're in. Move out to the street, carefully. You don't want to make me nervous."

Copper runs to the curb with us, wagging his tail. He probably thinks we're going for another ride.

We're going for a ride, all right.

The cop with the shotgun says, "You, the cunt, cross your fingers and put them on top of your head."

"You don't need to talk to her like that," I say. "What the hell's wrong with you? She's a lady."

"Yeah, I can tell. What house did she work in last?"

"You sonofabitch. If you didn't have that shotgun—"

"Yeah, I know. You're a big man. You'd jam it up my ass."

He laughs, clicking the hammer back when I drop my hands an inch or two. The sound's ominous.

"Reach for the moon."

"Okay, I'm reaching," I say.

<u>HARRY PIERPONT</u>

Long lines form along the corridor outside our cell. There must be several hundred people here to see the Dillinger gang.

John sits on the edge of his bed, hunched over. He's been shaking hands with people and signing autographs all afternoon. He told people to vote for Sheriff Belton the next time he runs for reelection.

John said, "Belton captured us when no one else could do it. He's your man."

Belton struts around with a six-shooter strapped to his hip. He wears cowboy boots and a ten-gallon hat, and his stomach sticks out over his silver belt buckle. The fat prick thinks he's living in the Old West.

"I never understood why they didn't call it the Pierpont gang," I say.

"You're too crabby," John says. "You've got to develop your personality."

"My personality's fine."

"While you were sulking yesterday, some kid from Texas who was arrested for being drunk and disorderly impersonated you. The kid collected money from the crowd in a tin cup while he shook hands and signed autographs. I didn't know what an exciting life you'd led until I listened to the kid."

"Balls."

"Makley kept egging the kid on. He'd say, 'Tell them about the time we shot it out with the cops in Grass Creek,' and the kid would say, 'Whew, that was a close one.'"

"I never heard of Grass Creek."

"The kid didn't know that. By the time he was done he'd made enough money to pay his fine and his lawyer, so they let him walk this morning."

"I don't want to hear about it," I say.

JOHN DILLINGER

I'm tired. Tired of all the attention, the questions.

Leach wants to extradite me to Indiana, but someone else wants me in Wisconsin.

I'm wanted in Ohio and Illinois. I'm probably wanted in Gin Gin, and I've never been to Australia.

I tell a reporter, "I don't want to go back to Indiana. Leach has it in for me, even though I saved his life once. Harry and I were walking along Capitol Avenue in Indianapolis when we realized the guy ahead of us was Leach. Harry was all for shooting him right there, but I stopped him."

"I wish you hadn't," Harry says.

"Leach has charged me with everything from strangling goldfish to stealing the socks off a blind man, but my conscience is clear. I stole from the bankers. They stole from the people. All we did was help raise the insurance rates."

I show the reporter my rabbit's foot and tell him, "I shot it out of season a couple of weeks ago in Mooresville. I guess I'm just a born criminal."

"I don't think there's such a thing as a 'born criminal.'"

I give him the rabbit's foot. "You take it. My luck's running out anyway."

BILLIE FRECHETTE

"Harry asked me to marry him and Sheriff Belton said he'd pay for the license, but I'm already married. It's embarrassing," Mary says, setting down the movie magazine she was reading.

"You never told Harry before?"

"What was the point? I wasn't in it for a marriage license. I already had one. Why would I want another? I just wanted to have a little fun. I never had any fun when I was married. My husband never took me anyplace, and the only thing he ever gave me was crabs."

I look out our cell window into the courtyard below. A retarded prisoner runs back and forth, flapping his arms, as if he's trying to fly. He's been doing it all day.

Mary said it must be an omen, but I don't believe in that stuff.

"Bird," he says, "bird."

Crazy people give me the creeps.

Mary says, "I don't think I'd get married again even if it were legal. I've been reading about all these movie stars, and it's amazing—the crummy lives they lead."

I wonder who cares about their lives, but I guess Mary does. She reads movie magazines all day.

"One of them shoved a beer bottle up his girlfriend's vagina," Mary says.

"Why would he do a thing like that?"

"He was drunk, I guess."

"I was around a lot of drunks before I met John, but none of them tried anything like that. The guy must have been a pervert."

"He weighed three hundred and twenty pounds and he was staying at this swanky hotel in San Francisco," Mary says, as if that explains the guy's behavior.

"What happened to her?"

"She died of a ruptured bladder, but nothing happened to the guy who did it. I guess he was too rich and famous."

"And they say John and Harry are criminals."

The retarded guy is still running back and forth in the courtyard while a deputy watches him, smiling.

People are weird.

"I wonder what happened to Copper," I say. "I really miss the little guy."

ROBERT G. ESTILL

"One reporter wrote, 'Dillinger has none of the look of a conventional killer,' but I'll tell you: He looks like a killer to me, and I've prosecuted a lot of them. That's why I want to bring him back to Indiana—to make sure he gets what he deserves.

"The reporter wrote, 'Given a little more time and a wider circle of acquaintances, one can see Dillinger might presently become the central figure in a nationwide campaign, largely female, to prevent his frying in the electric chair.'

"I think the reporter ought to tell that to the widow of Patrolman O'Malley, the officer Dillinger gunned down, and to O'Malley's children.

"The reporter claims Dillinger told Sheriff Belton, 'We're exactly like you cops. You have a profession—we have a profession. Only difference is you're on the right side of the law, we're on the wrong.' But policemen try to preserve order and save lives, whereas men like Dillinger defy the social order, robbing and looting, and they don't care if they take lives.

"When I get Dillinger back to Indiana, I'm going to see that he gets what he deserves: the electric chair."

JOHN DILLINGER

"I'm being framed for crimes I never even read about."

HARRY PIERPONT

"In the last few years of my life there's never been a day but that some incident hasn't occurred to make me hate the law. I suppose I'm what you'd call an abnormal mental case, a case for a psychiatrist. Maybe I am. But once I was normal. Place your own construction on what I've said."

JOHN DILLINGER

Sergeant Frank "Killer" Reynolds sits next to me in the backseat of the car, a submachine gun pointed at my heart.

They flew me from Tucson to Douglas in a Bellanca monoplane, then I was transferred to an American Airlines flight that touched down in Fort Worth, Dallas, and Little Rock before it landed at Midway Airport in Chicago.

The plane always seemed to be touching down, and there were huge crowds, waiting to get a look at me, lined up along the landing strips. Some people were holding signs that said FREE DILLINGER above their heads. It sounded like a good idea to me.

I was handcuffed and shackled and my back hurt. I told the stewardess it seemed cold in the plane, but what did I know? I'd never been on one before. She draped a blanket over my shoulders somewhere between Dallas and Little Rock. She told me her name was Marge Brennan, and she wondered if she could have my autograph.

It was hard to write with the cuffs on but I signed a small piece of paper—*For my friend, Marge Brennan, who gave me a blanket somewhere over Arkansas*—as the land darkened below us.

Harry and Makley are being taken to Ohio on the train, but at least Billie and Mary are free.

The last time I saw Billie she was sitting in the back of the courtroom as they led me out of it, chained. I stopped to kiss her as the guards tugged at me, the chains cutting into my flesh.

Billie was crying, but I told her, "Don't worry, I'll see you again somehow."

A guard laughed. "Yeah, in the death house. He can wave at you just before they pull the switch."

The bastards. The dirty bastards.

The only decent cops were the ones I met from Racine.

They asked if I'd sign a submachine gun I was supposed to have dropped when we robbed the bank there. I told them Harry said it was one of his favorite places, and he'd gone bowling there. They laughed when I wrote, *Crime doesn't pay, John Dillinger,* on the Thompson.

Now there's a Thompson pointed at my heart as the car heads toward the Indiana state line and Crown Point. There're thirteen cars in the procession.

I've never seen so many cops before.

"Killer" Reynolds told me there were thirty-two cops from Chicago and another twenty-nine troopers from Indiana, and they all had bulletproof vests, submachine guns, rifles, shotguns, and pistols, and they were all waiting for me to make a move. I asked if they had any poison gas, laughing, but he didn't think that was funny. I wonder what they think I'm going to do.

Reynolds says, "I have orders to kill you if anything goes wrong, anything at all. I want you to know that."

"Thanks."

"Nothin' would make me happier."

His face seems deformed, as if it were ruined by a pair of forceps at birth. His lower lip's twisted, so that he has a kind of perpetual sneer. I'll bet he tore the wings off butterflies when he was a kid, and that girls crossed to the other side of the hall when they met him in the corridors at school.

We should be in Crown Point, where they'll lock me in the Lake County Jail, in less than an hour.

I've been in jails before, and I got out before.

Reynolds says, "You know how many notches I have on my pistol?"

"No."

I never knew anyone who notched his gun before, not even Baby Face.

"Seven. They all thought they was hot potatoes, but I showed 'em."

"Hot potatoes, huh?"

"Yeah, I showed 'em good."

I can hear the tires humming on the asphalt. It's a lonely sound.

"Killer" nudges me with his Thompson.

"Well, John, why don't you try making a break? Don't you want to jump out of the car?"

"Why would I want to deprive myself of your company?" I ask. "You're a hell of a guy."

They remove my cuffs and shackles once we're inside the jail. Maybe they'd like to see me attempt an escape, but I'll disappoint them this time.

Sheriff Holley's a petite woman in her late thirties. She's standing next to the chief of police when I'm led into the dining area of the jail, and some state troopers are grouped behind them. They look as if nothing would make them happier than to kill me.

There must be fifty reporters in the room, most of them with cameras. It's a festive occasion. Someone even brought a couple of kegs of beer along, so no one will have to go thirsty.

I'm standing next to Holley and Estill when one of the reporters asks me, "How do you feel about Sheriff Holley?"

"She seems like a fine lady."

"How about Estill?"

"I like Estill."

"Even though he's vowed to send you to the electric chair?"

"I don't hold that against him. I know he's got a job to do, like anyone else."

"How about a picture of the three of you?"

I nod, standing closer to Estill, and the photographers start snapping pictures. Estill's wearing glasses with wire rims and a double-breasted suit with pinstripes. He probably belonged to a fraternity in college, and only went so far with his sweetheart. I'll bet he's never done an illegal thing in his life, and he's proud he's never chewed or smoked.

Someone yells, "Why don't you put your arm around Dillinger, Bob?" and I can feel Estill's hand on my left shoulder.

I lean against him, smiling, my right arm on his shoulder.

"I'll make you famous, Bob."

J. EDGAR HOOVER

"I was shocked at seeing newspaper photographs of a state's attorney who is about to prosecute a vicious criminal posing with his arm around the criminal's neck, both of them smiling and exhibiting friendship. For a state's attorney to put himself in such a familiar attitude with a criminal is to instill in the mind of the criminal the hope of avoiding the death penalty. Perhaps it isn't unethical, but it is certain that such familiarity breeds contempt for law enforcement in the minds of criminals. No picture has ever made me more angry."

JOHN DILLINGER

"You may think I'm soft because I'm a woman, but I'm not going to put up with any monkey business," Sheriff Holley says. There are dark circles under her eyes, and her shoulders are slumped. Her hair is brown and stringy. She must not have washed it in a week.

She watches me from the corridor outside my cell. She's always watching. At night she sleeps in a small room at the end of the hall, although the wing I'm in is supposed to be escape-proof. Nothing is.

"That sounds like a good title for a Marx Brothers film," I say, *"Monkey Business,"* but she doesn't laugh. Maybe she isn't a moviegoer.

"If you try to break out, or if your friends try to break you out, you'll be shot like a mad dog. I want you to understand that."

"Yeah, Deputy Reynolds kind of made it clear on the ride down here."

"The county commissioners appointed me to succeed my husband because they knew I could do the job. Roy had been a dentist in Gary before he became sheriff, but he was always depressed because no one likes dentists. They have the highest rate of suicide of any professional group in America, and he didn't want to end up killing himself. So he ran for sheriff and got elected. It seemed like a good idea at the time. But he was shot down by a madman seventeen days after the beginning of his second term. It's ironic, isn't it? Roy got into this line of work so he wouldn't die young."

BILLIE FRECHETTE

"I'm sorry, but you'll have to strip," Sheriff Holley says.

"It's all right. I haven't got anything you haven't seen before."

"Yeah. I used to see it all in the mirror every night, but I quit looking when I hit thirty-six. Suddenly, there was too much of it."

Holley touches her breasts in the bleak jailhouse light that casts no shadows. She's wearing olive-drab pants and a matching shirt. I think she gave up caring at some point, but there's still something feminine about her.

I put my skirt and blouse on a chair in the corner of the room that smells of chloride and ammonia. No one's seen me naked since I was released from jail in Tucson. My eyes water.

As I slide my underpants down my legs, Sheriff Holley looks away. I'd imagine working in a prison would make you hard.

"I guess you think I'm a dangerous character," I say.

I told Holley I'm John's wife.

"No, I'm just following the rules."

Holley picks up my blouse, turning it inside out, then she shakes my skirt, as if she were ready to hang it on the line to dry. She inspects my bra and panties. Satisfied.

Holley says, "You can get dressed now."

John and I are sitting across from each other at a small table that wobbles, but we're not allowed to touch each other.

My body aches.

There's a guard holding a submachine gun at the other end of the room—he keeps watching us while he chews gum—and I know there's another guard with another Thompson outside the door. And another. And another.

I speak so softly, leaning toward John, that I can still hear the guard chewing gum.

"If your lawyer's caught bringing you a wooden pistol, he can claim it's a joke. Piquett says there's no law against bringing a toy gun into jail. Holley wouldn't think it's funny, but she couldn't do much. Piquett's a fast talker."

"I'm paying him fifty thousand dollars, and he wants to bring me a wooden pistol?"

"He says he'll have to spend ten thousand to bribe all the guards."

"That makes me feel a lot better," John says. "How the hell am I supposed to escape with a wooden pistol?"

"Piquett says you'll think of something. He thinks you're resourceful."

The guard chews.

"It's nice to know Piquett has such faith in me. Maybe he thinks I can walk on water, too."

"He says the pistol's so well-made it'll fool anyone. It looks like the real thing."

"It's too bad it won't shoot like the real thing."

"Well, no setup's perfect," I say.

"Five more minutes," the guard with the Thompson says, looking our way.

"I still think my plan's best," John says.

"Everyone thinks his plan's best. It's human nature."

"Red and a couple of others could dynamite the southwest corner of the jail, blowing away the brickwork, then they could rush in here and cut through the bars with blowtorches. It wouldn't take more than a few minutes."

"Red wondered what the guards would be doing all that time. This place is a fortress."

John smiles. "Maybe you could walk down the street naked and distract them."

"Yeah, for all of five seconds. You've got to be realistic, John."

"It would distract *me*."

"I think Red's right. We'd better stick with Piquett's plan. Let him smuggle in the wooden gun."

JOHN DILLINGER

A middle-aged Negro named Herbert Youngblood's in the cell next to me. He looks like he could have been a heavyweight boxer, and his shaved head glistens like a bowling ball.

He says, "It's strange havin' a name like Youngblood

when you ain't young no more. When I was a pup, I never thought about bein' old. Other folks was old: The janitor at the junior high, the shoeshine boy, this sax player I knew. It was like a disease other people got. It wasn't gonna happen to me. Now I don't think about nothin' else. Probably 'cause I'se gonna die in the joint."

"Maybe not," I say.

"Yeah. I been found guilty of first-degree murder. Now I'se waitin' for what the judge say. I try to tell the po-lice it was self-defense, but they don't want to hear about it. I'se just another crazy nigger to them."

"Who'd you kill?"

"This Eye-talian guy named Nicosia who run a fruit stand in Gary. I bought this big, ol' watermelon from him one afternoon. I'se goin' out of his store when he say, 'You forgot to pay me, boy.' 'Man, you crazy,' I tol' him, but he say he gonna call the po-lice if I don't give him his melon back, and he pull this pistola, wavin' it at me.

"I drop the watermelon, *splat,* on the street, and grab the pistola. It's hot, rainy out. You can see the steam comin' up from the street while we were punchin' each other. Then there's this big *bang* and Nicosia, he fall down onto the sidewalk. His eyes are wide open, but you can tell he don't see nothin' no more. That's when the po-lice arrive. I'se standin' there in the rain holdin' the pistola, and they gonna fry me now."

"They haven't fried you yet," I say.

"That lawyer of yours, Mr. Picket, he seem like a smart fellow," Herbert says.

"At least he kept the judge from transferring me to Michigan City. I'd never get out of there."

"I don't think you be getting' out of here, neither. No offense, Mr. Dillinger. They say Houdini couldn't get out of Crown Point, and it sure look it to me."

"Appearances can be deceiving, Herbert."

Sam Cahoon staggers toward me, his eyes red, his hands shaking. His hair's wispy, and he hasn't shaved in a couple of days. He has a face like a brier patch.

A group of us are exercising in the corridor outside our cells. It's Saturday morning, and Sam's bringing us soap and towels for our Saturday night showers.

"You have a rough night, Sam?"

"Afraid so, John." He has a high-pitched, squeaky voice, and titters when he laughs. "But things are better than they used to be. My wife, God bless her, died a couple of years ago, so she isn't here to nag me about my drinkin' anymore. And they got tired of lockin' me up all the time, so they give me this job and fifty dollars a month. I always used to be on the inside lookin' out, but that's changed. At sixty-four I'm finally a free man."

I jam the wooden pistol into Sam's side when he hands me my soap and towel.

"Sam, I don't want to hurt you, but you're going to have to help me out. I'm going to be a free man, too, but I can't afford to wait till I'm sixty-four."

"I wouldn't wait that long if I had it to do over, but I was too drunk to know any better most of the time."

"You and I are going to take a little walk to the end of the corridor, and you're going to call Deputy Blunk for me, you understand?"

Sam nods and we go down the corridor together, Youngblood following a few steps behind, holding a handle he broke off from a mop. When we come to the stairway leading to the second floor, Sam opens the door with his key and yells, "Hey, Blunk, could you come up here a minute?"

I take Blunk's keys and pistol when he comes through

the door and tell Sam, "Blunk can keep Herbert company while you and I go downstairs." I like the feel of the .38 in my hand. "You can call Warden Baker for me."

"John, I can't do it."

"Then I guess Blunk will have to do it, while you stay with Herbert."

Youngblood puts a huge hand on Sam's shoulder, saying, "You and me be all right. We be buddies, won't we, Sam?"

I follow Blunk down the stairs to the second floor, nudging him in the left kidney with the barrel of the pistol.

"Call Warden Baker."

"What if I don't?"

"I'll be honest. I didn't like you when you booked me, and I still don't like you." He's one of those guys who enjoys doing his job too much. "Do I need to say more?"

"No, I get the picture."

Blunk's hands are shaking when he opens the door leading to the first floor. His fingers are ink-stained from booking the prisoners.

Blunk yells, "Hey, Lou, I need to see you."

I can hear Baker's footsteps echo in the stairway as he comes toward us. He'd been a jeweler before the Depression, and he liked to say, "I used to sell watches, now I watch cells." Then he'd laugh. But he doesn't laugh when I show him my pistol. He says, "You'll never get out of here."

"I know. I was killed up on the third floor, and this is all a bad dream."

"Being funny isn't going to get you past all the guards down below."

"No, but this pistol will help."

I lock Baker into the cell with Cahoon, then Herbert and I follow Blunk down the stairs to the first floor.

A trustee named Moore who thinks he's a poet is sitting at the desk outside the jail office. He has a full set of keys to the jail and a voice like a rusty file, and the wastebasket next to the desk is filled with crumpled paper.

I tap him on the shoulder with my pistol and say, "I hate to interrupt your work on an epic, but I need the keys, Todd."

A National Guardsman's dozing in a chair, a submachine gun resting on his lap when Herbert and I follow Moore and Blunk into the main office. I grab the machine gun, covering everyone, while Herbert takes another machine gun from a rack on the wall. Then he takes some ammunition from a cabinet beneath the gun rack.

"Well, lookie here." Herbert smiles.

Blunk and I wait in the main office while Herbert locks Moore and the Guardsman into a cell on the second floor, then the three of us go through the laundry room to the alley behind the prison.

It's raining.

The water must be four inches deep, swirling around our ankles as we head toward the back door to the Main Street garage. It's only a hundred yards, but it seems further.

At least most people will stay home in this weather.

We slosh our way through the water, walking with our heads down, the rain pelting us. I can feel the water running down my back, soaking my shirt, but I stay close to Blunk, holding the machine gun.

I'm not going back.

A mechanic's working on an old Packard, bending over the engine, when we enter the garage.

Three other cars are parked along the far wall: a Buick, a Terraplane, and a Ford.

"Which one runs the best?" I ask.

"The V-eight Ford." The mechanic doesn't bother to look up. "Mrs. Holley's car."

"Where're the keys to it?"

"In the ignition. Where do you think they'd be?"

The concrete floor's oily, and I can hear the rain on the tin roof. It's a blue sound.

The mechanic looks up, annoyed. ED is stitched on the pocket of his striped overalls. He could be a convict.

"You're going to take a little ride with us, Ed."

"I can't go," he says. "I'm working on a car." Then he notices my submachine gun. "Jesus."

"It's Dillinger," Blunk says. "Him and the colored guy broke out of jail."

Herbert says, "I'se always the nigger when I'se locked up, but now I'se the colored guy. Pretty soon they be callin' me 'Mr. Youngblood.' I could get to like this."

I tell Blunk, "You drive," getting into the front seat next to him while Herbert and Ed get in back. The car rocks as Herbert shifts his weight.

"I'm going under protest," Ed says. "I don't like this. I want you to know that. I don't like it one bit."

"Ah, shut up," Blunk says. He narrowly misses a passing car as he heads north on Main Street, the rain beating against the windshield. "Nobody gives a shit what you like."

When we pass the First National and Commercial Banks, I say, "I'd rob one of them if we weren't in a hurry. We could use a little extra cash."

"I like that," Herbert says. "Maybe we make a withdrawal next time." I can see the whites of his eyes in the rearview mirror and his teeth.

I tell Blunk to take the first gravel road past the Pennsylvania Railroad tracks when we come to the edge of town. We'll work our way west until we pick up Route 41, then we'll head north toward Illinois and freedom. I wonder if this is how the darkies felt when they headed north during the Civil War.

135

I begin to sing, "Get along, little dogie, get along. You're heading toward the last roundup."

"I always thought it was 'git along,'" Blunk says.

It's still raining when the car skids off the muddy road into a ditch. I twist the red light from the front of the Ford so we won't be as conspicuous while Blunk and Ed heave the car back onto the road. Heavy dark clouds hover overhead, and the sky has the texture of soiled wallpaper. I throw the red light into a field that used to grow something before it flooded. We'll take root if we stand here much longer.

Herbert covers them with the muddy barrel of his machine gun. He keeps blinking as the rain runs off his shaved head. "Now I know how those guards be feelin' when they watch them cotton-pickin' niggers on the chain gang."

I show Blunk the wooden pistol I used to get the drop on him and Cahoon when we get back into the car. I don't think I'll ever be warm or dry again.

"You wouldn't think a guy could make a break with a peashooter like this, would you? But I did it all with my little toy pistol."

"I don't want to hear about it," Blunk says.

I tell Blunk to stop the car at Lilley's Corner, about two miles from the Illinois border. A sodden cow stands in a field across the road, watching us with its big sad eyes, and there's an abandoned diner with broken windows and a rusting sign out front. Lilley's. The owner must have died a hundred years ago.

"This is where you and Ed get out," I say.

Blunk's been all right.

"Is this where you gun us down?"

"I've never gunned anyone down."

"Sure, that's why you were in jail."

"I was in jail for robbing banks. They made up the other stuff."

It's almost stopped raining when we get out of the car. Blunk and Ed can walk into Peotone, then catch a bus back to Crown Point.

I shake their hands, then give them four dollars for bus fare.

"I'd give you guys more, but that's all I can spare. I've only got fifteen. But I'll remember you at Christmas."

"Sure, you and Santy Claus," Blunk says, but he looks relieved.

I tell Herbert, "You sit in back again so you can crouch down when we hit the main roads. Even the cops might think there's something suspicious about me driving a colored person around."

"I been in back of the bus a whole bunch of times, but I never been chauffered around by no white man befo', Mr. Dillinger. Now I know what they be talkin' about when they call someone a big nigger," Herbert says as we cross the border into Illinois.

SHERIFF LILLIAN HOLLEY

There must be a hundred reporters jammed into the room, and they all want to know how Dillinger escaped.

They've rigged up half a dozen microphones, and my voice sounds raspy coming through the speakers. Even the Movietone news people are here. The bright lights are blinding, and I can hear the cameras whirring. Whirring.

The room smells of linseed oil and sweaty bodies, and I think I'm going to be sick. It's worse than those mornings I woke up vomiting when I was pregnant. The reporters' voices roar and build inside my head until I think my eardrums will burst. I swallow hard, trying to relieve the pressure, but it doesn't help.

I say, "Dillinger took one chance in a million, and all the breaks were with him and against me. Ordinarily, I would have walked out of this room and into the jail about the time he was making his escape. In the six weeks he's been here, I've stayed on the job until three A.M., then I'd try to sleep five or six hours."

I stare into the bright eye of the camera, blinking. I must look like I'm ready to cry. Next week I'll see myself on the screen of the Mystic Theatre and cringe.

"I was dressing when a trustee ran into my room with a shotgun and said, 'Dillinger's escaped.' I thought he'd gone mad at first. He said, 'Have you got a gun here? I can't shoot with this thing.' I handed him my pistol and said, 'Kill him,' but it was too late.

"Too late." My voice echoes through the speakers, and I clutch the microphone, feeling faint.

"I don't know how any of it happened. This jail's supposed to be escape-proof."

A reporter in the front row asks, "Before the escape, you said you could handle everything, and now Dillinger's gone. Will you admit this job's too big for a woman now?"

"Oh, hell's fire," I say, "of course not," but I can feel the phlegm rising in my throat and my voice breaks.

JOHN DILLINGER

I let Herbert out in front of a pool hall when we get to Chicago. The opaque windows haven't been washed in years.

Herbert says, "I'se gonna get some money, then find a big, fat high-yellow woman to help me exercise my jones. Then the two of us gonna order up some barbecue from the Rib Shack. I likes my ribs the way I likes my women, with plenty of meat on 'em."

I give Herbert a five-dollar bill after we shake hands. I say, "I know it isn't much, but maybe it'll get you going."

"I can't take your money, Mr. Dillinger."

"Sure you can, Herbert."

A colored woman shakes a frozen sheet in the fierce wind blowing off the lake. She leans out of a third-story window from a tenement across the street.

The sheet snaps, almost tearing itself from her fingers, as she tries to drape it over the rusted fire escape that serves as a clothesline. Then she leans farther out, the sheet billowing.

The lives of the poor are unimaginable. I know why so many of them voted for the Communist candidate for president in '32. He talked about equal distribution of the wealth and gave them hope, but it blew away.

I ran home crying one windy day like this when I was five and my kite shattered against the red brick of the elementary school. I never liked winter after that.

"I hope you find that high-yellow woman, Herbert."

"When I do, I tell her my buddy Mr. Dillinger give me the money for our good time, but I know she won't be believin' me. High-yellow women be like that. They don't believe nothin'."

BILLIE FRENCHETTE

"It's true," Piquett says, "John escaped from Crown Point this morning. He broke out with the wooden pistol."

Piquett talked to Warden Baker a few minutes ago.

"They'll kill John," I say. "The cops won't let him get away."

Piquett's short and stocky and his gray hair's combed into a three-inch pompadour. Maybe he thinks it makes him look taller. He's wearing an expensive double-breasted gray suit, and he could be a corrupt police commissioner or a successful thug.

"John took Sheriff Holley's car when he escaped," Piquett says. "I think that's priceless." His laughter's throaty.

Raindrops splatter against the windows. The stores along the street below look blurred, but we've been drinking all afternoon. Maybe it's the gin.

Piquett says, "I rented this office because it was on the top floor. It gives me a sense of satisfaction to look down on things. I think it has something to do with my childhood. My father was a blacksmith who lost everything when the horse and buggy disappeared, and he was too old to learn another trade. There were nine children and almost no money, so I was never able to attend law school. I'd dreamed of going to Stanford, but I taught myself the law while I waited on tables and tended bar." He laughs. "I spent many an hour in bars, but it took me more than twelve tries to pass the bar."

He shrugs, sipping his drink. "Beer was the only beverage I could afford as a young man. Maybe that's why I have such an appreciation for the taste of juniper berries. London dry gin represented a step up for me. A better life."

"I jus' wanna see Johnnie," I say.

JOHN DILLINGER

I don't know why I get headaches if I go more than a day without sex. Some women have accused me of using that as an excuse to get them into bed, but the pain's real and I don't need an excuse.

I tell Billie, "You have magic fingers" when she touches me, but other things are magical, too.

I made love to a girl in a cemetery once. We held hands, stumbling on tombstones in the dark. Clouds slid across the moon.

I told her, "It's a night when the dead rise up out of their graves."

"You shouldn't scare me," she said.

Other things rose up, too.

She was a timid, lonely girl from a small mining town. When she was growing up, she'd look down toward the coke kilns built along the river and watch the barges go by.

She described the company houses and the dusty park where the kids played, where they'd sneaked their first cigarettes.

Her first sex was in the backseat of a Ford with a boy whose breath smelled of beer. When she bled on the upholstery, the boy said, "Jeez, my father will kill me."

I remember another time, driving across Nebraska. I stopped for a hot dog at a small café. A woman wearing a white dress walked by the window. She had white gloves, a white purse, and a white parasol, and I watched her round the corner.

The waitress told me she got off duty in an hour, and she wanted to show me something. I followed her into a cornfield at the edge of town, looking for the woman in white.

The waitress said she wanted to run away, that she'd been saving her money, but she was afraid to go. She'd heard you dropped off the edge of the earth a few miles west of Wahoo.

"The earth isn't flat," I said.

"Of course it is. That's one thing you're sure of when you grow up in Nebraska."

She asked me to take my pants off, then she inspected my penis, bending over it. "You could paint a face on its tip. With lipstick." And she did. Then she knelt before me. There in the late Nebraska afternoon. I felt her lips moving. The sun glinted on her freckles, and I touched her auburn hair.

I wondered if she did that for all the travelers who passed, or if she knew who I was. Maybe she'd drive past the field years later and tell a friend, "I was with John Dillinger there."

It was strange trying to imagine what she did on other afternoons when she was lonely.

I hold Billie, tightly.

There was ice on the windowpanes of our hotel room when we got out of bed one morning. Billie had a sore throat so I went outside, warming up the car, scraping the ice from the windshield, my feet sliding on ice.

Billie looked worried, squinting, watching me from the window of our room. Her breath condensed on the glass until it frosted over, but I knew she was there, watching.

Each piece of ice I scraped was for her.

The most wanted man in America.

I remembered: building a snowman one winter afternoon. I put a carrot where his penis should be. We'd just moved to Mooresville, and I didn't have many friends.

A neighbor said my snowman was obscene, that it would offend his daughter, who was a cheerleader in high school. She had long blond hair and large breasts that jiggled when she ran.

I laughed at him, but the snowman was demolished when I got up the next morning and someone had even taken the carrot.

"And they say you're a thief," Billie says. "You never stole a carrot from a kid."

We can see the bank from the window of our room at the Lincoln Hotel.

It won't be long now, maybe another hour, and we'll be walking into Security National to make a withdrawal.

Big news in Sioux Falls.

Van Meter lights a cigarette, coughing. His chest rattles, as if he were tubercular. I used to think Homer was skinny because he almost never ate when we were in Michigan City, but he's still gaunt, over six feet tall, 130 pounds at best. Maybe he does have TB.

Red watches Baby Face pace the room and says, "I haven't seen you in so long I thought you were dead."

"I ain't dead," Baby Face says. "I was workin' for Joe Parenti in this little town north of San Francisco. They called it the Egg Basket of the World because there was all these chickens. I never saw so many chickens. Peckin' and scratchin' and shittin'. It was somethin'. Parenti needed someone who was good with a gun."

"Why? Was someone killin' his chickens?" Homer asks.

I remember watching Homer grab flies out of the air in Michigan City. He'd throw his back out of joint and hobble around like a paralytic, the fly tied to a piece of thread. Even the guards were afraid of him.

"Parenti didn't have no goddamn chickens. He was one of the biggest bootleggers on the coast, but he had to look for another line of work when Prohibition ended, and I got tired of waitin' for him to make up his mind.

"He got weird at the end. He went around sayin' things like, 'Why do I open the door whenever darkness leans against it?' then he'd look at you like he expected an answer. I never knew what the fuck he was talkin' about."

"Wops are like that," Red says. "I worked with some on the coast. I don't know what was worse, tryin' to figure out what they were talkin' about or the weather in California. It never changed. All summer long, it was nothin' but sunshine. I started wishin' it would rain just to break the monotony."

"It's got to be better than Oklahoma," Homer says. "I was down there with Pretty Boy Floyd in Sallisaw. The Okies were always complaining about something—the banks, the drought, President Roosevelt—but, except for Floyd, they didn't do anything about it."

143

"You know what the hardest ten years in an Okie's life are?" Baby Face asks. He probably weighs as much as Homer, but he's half-a-foot shorter.

"I was only there a couple of weeks. How would I know?"

"Third grade," Baby Face laughs.

"I don't get it."

"It takes an Okie ten years to pass third grade."

"I don't think that's funny," Homer says.

"You don't think nothin's funny. That's your problem. You ain't got a sense of humor."

"I think we ought to go in blasting," Baby Face says. His eyes are yellow-and-slate gray, and he blinks in the March wind as we go up the steps to the bank.

"We don't shoot anyone unless we have to," I say. "I'm leading this gang. If you don't like that, you can find someone else to work with."

"It was just a suggestion."

Baby Face, Homer, and I hide our Thompsons under our overcoats.

Red leans against the Packard, a yellow muffler wrapped around his neck. He whistles feebly.

The sky's marble.

When we go into the bank Baby Face yells, "This is a holdup! Everyone on the floor!"

One of the clerks looks at the floor distastefully, as if he's afraid his suit will get dirty. Then he sits down slowly, hesitantly, before lying on his back.

Baby Face kicks him and says, "Facedown on the floor, stupid," while Homer cleans out the tellers' cages.

I put the large bills from the vault into a canvas sack.

Baby Face is hopping around, pointing his machine gun every which way because someone set the alarm off.

"Who did that?" he yells. "Who the hell did that?"

144

"What difference does it make?" Homer asks as we leave the bank.

Baby Face fires over the heads of some people who are standing across the street in front of a five-and-dime.

"I hate gawkers," he says and laughs when the glass in the front window shatters. Then he fires another burst at a cop car rounding the corner.

We're flanked by four women. Their dresses ruffle in the wind as we cross the sidewalk to the Packard. The women stand on the running boards once we get into the car. One of them yells, "Whee!" as if she thinks we're going on a picnic, but the others purse their lips, looking at the jagged sky. It's too cold for a picnic.

Homer tells them, "Hold onto your hats, ladies. We're going for a ride," as Red guns the car.

"They don't have no hats!" Baby Face yells.

"Don't be obsessed by details," Homer says. "I hate people who are anal-retentive."

He was always reading psychology when he was in Michigan City. Homer claimed he wanted to know where he went wrong.

"Are you callin' me an asshole?"

A bald-headed guy wearing bib overalls fires a shotgun blast into the radiator of the Packard as we drive by Antler's Pharmacy. There's a nude mannequin in the window next to a huge sign that says RUPTURED? TRY ONE OF OUR TRUSSES. Farmers must come from miles around, their faces bleached with pain, trying to keep their guts from falling into their testicles, bent over, holding themselves.

"Shit," Homer says, looking at the steam rising from the radiator, and the ladies begin to scream.

Baby Face laughs some more, a mad Rumpelstilskin, as he throws roofing nails onto the highway. "That ought to slow the cops down," he says. We've lost sight of them by the time the Packard dies on a country road.

The ladies stand next to the car, trying to stay out of the wind, shivering, and I flag down a farmer in a new Dodge who's heading toward town.

I tell the farmer, "We need to borrow your car, but you can stay with the ladies."

"What if I don't want to loan you my car?" the farmer asks. One of his front teeth is missing and the rest are tobacco-stained. He's wearing a blue peacoat that's too small for him, and I wonder if he was in the navy.

When I show him my .45 he says, "Sure, sure, anything to be cooperative. I don't much care for banks myself."

Homer and Red give the ladies their coats, but Baby Face says, "I'm not givin' my coat to no dame I'll never see again."

I give the other two ladies my overcoat and jacket, then shake hands with the farmer before we head east toward the state line and Minnesota.

"Didn't the nuns teach you any manners?" Homer asks. He taps Baby Face on the shoulder.

The sky's clouding up, and it's ready to rain again. Large bugs with yellow blood splatter against the windshield.

"My manners are fine," Baby Face says. "I never chew gum when I'm with some dame."

"What a prince," Homer says.

"You're fuckin' A. Sister Veronica called me her little angel 'cause I never farted in church, like most of them kids in the convent, and I always learned my catechism. The other kids, they was always getting' their hands hit with a ruler 'cause they was pullin' their puds or somethin' when they was supposed to be helpin' the sisters."

"I still think you should have given those ladies your overcoat," Homer says.

———

"I wonder if they really shave their heads," Homer asks.

Baby Face leans back against the seat, half-asleep. "Who?"

"The nuns."

"How should I know?" Baby Face asks. "I never saw Sister Veronica without her habit."

Red says, "I heard they shave their pussies."

"Why the hell would they do that?" Baby Face asks. "Nobody's lookin' at 'em."

"Maybe the pope tells them to," Red says. "Maybe it's got somethin' to do with obedience."

"Yeah, maybe it's papal," Homer says.

"Why would he tell 'em somethin' like that?" Baby Face asks.

"You tell me," Red says. "I'm not a Catholic."

BILLIE FRECHETTE

John sets the paper down, then gets up from the kitchen table.

"They got Herbert," he says, standing in front of the window overlooking St. Paul. He's silhouetted against the sooty morning sky, his shoulders rounded.

"When? Where?"

"In Port Huron. Michigan." John's voice is soft. "Last night."

"I'm sorry."

"Yeah. Me, too."

I wait for him to continue.

"Herbert flashed a big bankroll, according to the paper, and someone tipped the cops. He'd been in and out of the colored bars in Port Huron."

John puts his hands in his pockets, standing in front of the window. The smoke from a thousand chimneys rises into the sickly sky.

147

"They thought they'd disarmed him, but Herbert had a second gun on him. The bastards shot him seven times, but it took him four hours to die. . . . Billie, it'll happen to me."

"No, it won't, John. You're not going to die for a long time."

I can smell the bay rum he uses as an aftershave when I stand next to him. It has a clean scent and it comes from the West Indies.

It's good touching him.

"They kept asking where I was, and Herbert told them he'd been with me the night before. They blockaded every road within miles of Port Huron, but they figure I escaped into Canada."

"They never know where you are, John. Will Rogers even joked about it on the radio. He said, 'The police had Dillinger surrounded in Chicago, but he robbed a bank in Sioux Falls that day. They were right on his trail. Just three states behind.'"

John laughs.

"Herbert said he wanted to find a high-yellow woman the last time I saw him. I hope he found her before the cops killed him."

"I hope he did, too," I say.

SPRING 1934

My attorney makes an impassioned plea for mercy, saying, "I now leave the fate of Harry Pierpont in your hands. I know God is with me, with the defendant, in the hearts of every one of you. So I hand Harry over to you, and I pray God in His goodness will show you the way to do the right thing."

The jury is only out for forty-five minutes, and I'm sentenced to death.

My mother's crying when I'm led out of the courtroom, and my father sits beside her, his head bowed, beaten—old.

National Guardsmen armed with loaded rifles, pistols, machine guns, and riot sticks line the halls in case John tries to break me out. My arms and legs are shackled, and the Guardsmen stand at attention in their uniforms. I know John would break me out if he could, but it's hopeless.

When I hobble past Makley's cell he asks, "What was the verdict?"

"What do you think?"

Harry yells, "Good luck, Charley," as I'm led out of the cell block, but I'll need more than luck.

When the prosecuting attorney asks how I spell my last name, I say, "It's been so long since I used my right name that I don't know. You look up the record."

I'm accused of being a wise guy, but I'm just tired of answering questions.

151

They keep asking me about John and I tell them, "He's the kind of guy anyone would be glad to have for a brother. I'd rather get the hot seat than see him caught."

The jury deliberates for three-and-a-half hours, then finds me guilty of murder in the first degree. They claim I'm not repentant, and it's true. I'd do it all over again.

When I'm led past Harry's cell he asks, "What did they give you?"

"Everything," I say.

<u>JOHN DILLINGER</u>

"Harry was always a good boy," Mrs. Pierpont says. "It isn't fair."

She and I sit on the porch swing at the farmhouse where Harry grew up, and I try to imagine him skipping stones across the creek or catching polliwogs in the quart jars his mother used to pickle cucumbers. One summer he had a lemonade stand at the side of the road, and now he's waiting to die in the electric chair.

Mrs. Pierpont's white socks are rolled at the ankles, and the plaid jacket she's wearing is too big for her.

We sit, swinging, as the sky darkens and bats fly out of the loft above the red barn.

"I'd break him out if I could," I say, "but there're too many guards."

"I know."

"It would be suicide."

Mrs. Pierpont nods. "It's funny. Harry always worried if a black cat crossed his path, and he wouldn't walk under a ladder. I used to tell him it was silly to be superstitious, but they sentenced him to die on Friday the thirteenth. Maybe he wasn't so silly after all."

MARY KINDER

I tell the reporters to go away, but they keep asking me to make a statement.

Finally, I go out onto the porch.

I say, "I had a good experience. I don't regret a bit of it," then I go back into the house, pulling the shades in the front room. I sit there in the dim light, smoking, waiting for the reporters to leave.

BILLIE FRECHETTE

"Someone's at the door," I say.

John rolls over onto his side, facing me, his cheeks shadowed.

"What time is it?"

"I don't know. Early." I get out of bed, rubbing my eyes. I squint at the Big Ben on the bureau. The guy at the furniture store said it was made out of "faux" mahogany. Most things are fake these days. "Nine-fifteen."

"For Christ sake."

When the knocking continues I put on the blue negligee John gave me for my birthday.

"I'll get it."

John nods as I fasten the latch chain, then open the door a couple of inches.

Two men I've never seen are in the hall. Their shirts are made out of oxford cloth, but they're sweating.

I don't like it.

Summer's almost three months away.

"Is Carl Hellman here?"

It's the name John's been using in St. Paul.

"My husband ought to be back this afternoon," I say.

"Maybe we can talk to you," the older man says. He's wearing a gray hat with a stained brim.

"I think you ought to come back this afternoon."

"I think you ought to let us in."

"You'll have to wait a minute until I put some clothes on," I say, shutting the door, double-locking it.

When I go back into our room, John's sitting on the edge of our bed, tying his shoes.

"Hurry up," I say. "The cops are here."

JOHN DILLINGER

The bullets from my submachine gun knock the door off its hinges, then Billie and I go out into the empty hallway.

It's filled with splintered wood and broken bits of plaster, and you can see the laths and chicken wire where the plaster used to be. We choke on the dust and formaldehyde.

Anyone standing in front of the door would have been cut to pieces, but no one's there.

Billie drags two suitcases over the worn carpet toward the back stairway, and I follow her, holding the Thompson.

Someone yells, "Stop, hold it!" as I reach the top of the stairs.

The bullets from my Thompson tear huge holes in the ceiling, shattering the light bulbs and breaking a window at the far end of the hall, and I remember what it was like working in the upholstery shop. Particles of dust hung in the thin air, and my hands bled from the fibers.

I see the flash from a pistol and feel something tear into

my leg before I hear the shot, but I make it down the stairs, limping, into the alley.

Billie slips, falling, her right knee hitting the wet cobblestones. She drops the suitcases, but picks herself up quickly, running through the open doorway to the garage where the Hudson's parked.

I can hear the engine turning over, then the car's coming toward me down the narrow alley littered with broken bottles, oil cans, and empty cardboard boxes, mushy from the rain.

I throw the suitcases into the backseat, then get in beside Billie as two men come out of the apartment house. They're running with their arms out, holding pistols—firing—and the bullets ricochet off the side of the car as Billie accelerates and we round the corner. She must be doing fifty by the time we reach Lexington Avenue.

Billie turns to me, smiling. Then she notices the blood on my pants and begins to cry.

"You're hit, John. The bastards shot you."

The car swerves as she takes a corner too quickly, wiping away tears, the tires squealing.

"I can't see where I'm going because of the goddamn tears," she says, driving with one hand.

She almost never swears.

"It's nothing Doc Kuhns won't be able to fix," I say. "Just keep the car on the road, and I'll tell you how to get there."

BILLIE FRECHETTE

"The bullet passed through the fleshy portion of his lower left leg. See, here," Doc says, pointing. His hands shake. "He'll be fine."

Doc discusses John's condition as if he were in another

155

room. Maybe Doc thinks John's senses are dulled by the pain and the drugs.

"You're sure?"

"Of course I'm sure. I've been treating patients for almost forty years now. No offense, John, but some of them were a lot more famous than you."

John nods as Doc bandages the wound.

We came to Mrs. Salt's Nursing Home, where Doc spends most of his time treating patients for venereal diseases when he isn't performing abortions. There is no Mrs. Salt, but there's a Mrs. Gervasoni, who's related to Lucky Luciano, Doc says.

John gave him a thousand dollars in cash, and Doc stuffed the roll of bills into his right front pocket.

"Aren't you going to count it?" John asked.

"Why should I?" Doc asked. "It's either all there or it isn't."

"That's an interesting way to look at things," John said.

"If we're going to survive as a species, we've got to learn to trust each other," Doc said. "Two things are imperative in life: friendship and trust. Aside from a few medical tricks I've picked up, that's all I've learned in almost seventy years." His hair's gray, and he thinks he's a philosopher.

John's sweating, and I wipe his forehead with a damp washcloth Mrs. Gervasoni gave me.

Doc says, "I treated Frank James and Cole Younger when they were old men, and I was startin' out in Kansas City. You could tell they'd been somebody once. They were the real thing: desperadoes."

Doc's wire-rimmed glasses glint in the light as he secures the bandages.

"I met Frank," John says.

"What was he like?" I ask.

John pauses, squinting, as if he's trying to remember.

Maybe the pain is finally getting to him. "Doc's right," he says, "you could tell he'd been somebody once."

JOHN DILLINGER

"I was eleven the summer Pa took me to the James Farm. Frank was an old man dressed in black. At first I thought he was an undertaker.

"'In a way, I guess I was,' Frank chuckled, standing next to the fence in front of the farm; there was a sign nailed to it: KODAKS BARRED.

"I asked, 'How many men did you kill?' before Pa said, 'That's not a polite question,' but Frank said, 'It wasn't a polite time,' and smiled.

"Even at eleven, I knew most men's lives didn't amount to much. Knew there were men called 'soldiers' killing each other in a war across the ocean, although I wasn't sure what an ocean was. Pa said it was even bigger than Lake Superior.

"I pointed a make-believe pistol at some people coming up the road and yelled, *'Bam bam bam bam bam!'* as fast as I could so it almost sounded like the Thompson I got later.

"Mr. James put an arm around me, smiling.

"Someday I was going to be a famous outlaw, my photo in every newspaper in America, and I wished someone were there to take a picture of the two most dangerous men alive."

PENNY HANCOCK

"Take my picture," Uncle Johnnie says.

He's holding the wooden pistol he used to break out of Crown Point and a submachine gun, and he's smiling. He's wearing a three-piece suit, a shirt with a button-down collar and a natty-looking tie. Except for the guns, he could be the head of the Chamber of Commerce, but he came home for the family picnic.

I asked why he didn't change into something more casual, but he said it never hurts to look sharp. He's always comfortable, unless there's a cop nearby.

It's the kind of Sunday afternoon they must have in heaven.

The sun's shining, and I can feel things growing, pushing their way up through the moist earth. My mom and dad are laughing, drinking lemonade, and Grandpa's sampling the potato salad with his fingers. He laughs, *"He he he,"* because he thinks no one's looking.

Uncle Johnnie leans against the side of the house in the sunlight, and I watch him through the viewfinder of the Kodak.

"Take lots of pictures," Johnnie says.

He leans the Thompson against the back steps so he can put his arm around Billie. Her dark hair hangs to her shoulders, and he smiles when he says, "I'm going to marry this woman."

Then he sings a few bars from "All I Do Is Dream of You," his voice as warm as the sunlight.

"After Penny takes the photos, I want to eat another piece of that coconut-cream pie, Sis." He claims Mom's cooking is what really brought him back home. "And some more fried chicken."

"And he'll want a hot dog before he goes to bed," Billie says. "He always wants a hot dog before bedtime."

"All I Do Is Dream of You," Uncle Johnnie sings.

I keep snapping pictures.

Mom says, "I'll make you some pies to take with you. And some more fried chicken."

Uncle Johnnie hugs her.

"Thanks, Sis. You've done enough."

Mom begins to cry while Grandpa Dillinger pats Billie

on the back. He says, "Audrey, she'll give you her recipe for coconut-cream pie and fried chicken so Johnnie won't eat so many of them hot dogs. There's no tellin' what they put in them."

Grandpa's crying, too.

It's that kind of an afternoon.

Uncle Johnnie goes into the house when a plane circles the yard, slowly. We all know the FBI is looking for him, but Mom doesn't think they'd expect him to return to Mooresville.

"Even if they did," she says, "I don't think they'd want to come after him at the farm. It would be a terrible thing to shoot him down in front of us."

"Uncle Johnnie doesn't think it would bother Hoover," I say, then I go into the house.

I put Mercurochrome on Uncle Johnnie's wound, then we walk toward the woods, holding hands. He limps slightly, and he has a .45 tucked under his belt.

"You believe what's in the papers if you want to, but take it from me, I haven't killed anyone, and I hope I never have to," he says. "Take everything you hear about me with half a grain of salt, believe half of what's left, and there might be some truth in it."

I've never held hands with anyone who has a loaded .45 under his belt. It's like something you'd see in a movie.

Sometimes I wonder if the movies imitate life or if life imitates the movies.

Uncle Johnnie and I are still holding hands when we go into the woods, but he's whistling "For All We Know."

JOHN DILLINGER

The letters are in a box in the attic along with my bronzed baby shoes and a wrapper from a package of Kiss Me gum. I don't know why anyone would have saved the wrapper, but we hold on to strange, fragile things sometimes. I remember Dad scolded me when I gave a package to a girl who came into his store in Indianapolis, puckering my lips. Dad said I'd give anything away to someone with a pretty face.

Nothing has changed.

I can hear Billie and Sis laughing in the yard below.

There's a wasp nest in the corner, and I remember being stung on my thigh by a yellow jacket while I was burning rubbish behind the house one summer. It had flown up beneath the cuffs of my Levi's, and I jumped out of my pants there in the yard, running into the kitchen, crying, "Sis, sis," in my underwear. I must have been five or six, and it was one of the last times I cried.

I didn't cry when my father spanked me for tying a rope from our neighbor's outhouse to a freight train one Halloween. I'd gone to his house, trick-or-treating, and Mr. Simms said, "Trick, you little bastard," and dumped beer into my sack.

I laughed when the train went by, jerking the two-holer from the ground. I wished Mr. Simms were in it. Pieces of wood were strewn along the track, and there was shit everywhere.

Dad told me, "That was wrong, son," but he was trying not to laugh as his hand came down on my unrepentant bottom.

I take the letters out of the box, looking at them where the light comes through the louvers to let the heat escape. I'm sweating, even though I'm only wearing a T-shirt.

The paper's crinkled and the ink's faded, but I know what the letter says. *Dear Penny, I wish I could be there to spend Christmas with you*—there was a maggot in my stew and the pudding was rancid today—*but I'll be out sometime, and I intend to stay out. I can hardly believe you're old enough to have a beau.* I could hear the screams of the young man who was sodomized last night while the prison choir sang, "Away in a Manger." It was Christmas Eve. *I'm sorry to hear Sis isn't any better. She wants me to pray for her to get well, but I'm not very strong for praying. I think it will take more than prayers for her to get well or, for that matter, for me to get out of here. If anyone deserves health and happiness, it's your mother, so I'll try and pray for her, not that I think it will do any good.* The kid who was sodomized was taken to the infirmary this morning, bleeding from the rectum, while the prison chaplain told us God is love. After dinner, the warden passed out cigars. *Don't think I'm an atheist, I'm not, but God's ways seem strange to me sometimes.*

I put the letters and the Kiss Me wrapper back into the box, then I go downstairs and out onto the porch, where sun and shadow meet.

EMMETT HANCOCK

I ask Johnnie where he and Billie are going when they leave the farm and he says, "Let me tell you something. If you don't know anything, you can't tell anything, can you?"

"No."

"Let that be a lesson to you, then."

Sometimes I don't understand Johnnie.

JOHN DILLINGER

Billie and I are putting our suitcases into the car when I see a woman walking along the road in front of the house.

She's wearing a white dress with matching white gloves,

a white purse and shoes, and she's twirling a white parasol. She looks at me, smiling, as she passes the broken gate leading up to the house and I smile back, waving. I feel as if I've spent a lifetime waving at her.

It's late afternoon, and her elongated shadow follows her like an unwelcome acquaintance.

I know I've seen her before.

I run down the driveway to the road, but she's gone by the time I get there, as if she were absorbed by the sunlight.

When I get back to the car, Billie asks, "What was that all about?"

"Didn't you see the woman go by?"

"What woman?"

"She was dressed in white."

"It's getting to be that time of year. You know. Maybe she was going to a wedding. Or coming back from one."

"Yeah, that must be it," I say.

BILLIE FRECHETTE

"Something's wrong," I say. "I can feel it."

John parks the car across the street from Gilardi's Tavern on North State Street.

"You're always feeling things." John laughs. Except for the times we've been in bed, I've never seen him this happy.

It's been less than twenty-four hours since we left the farm. John crouched behind the front seat, a blanket thrown over him, while I drove, but his fuzzy voice came through the blankets.

He was singing "Hey, Hey, How Am I Doin'?" and I said, "Oh, be quiet," thinking of the times he'd sung it when he was winning at cards or dancing the carioca at the Chez Paree; he'd beg the orchestra leader to play it again and again, and we were always the first to begin dancing when the music started because

John liked us to be the only couple on the floor so everyone could see us step. He sang it at Riverside Park while he knocked over the targets at the shooting gallery; the customers lined up to watch him knock over the metal ducks that seemed to swim by. Even a cop watched him one day and John said, "I bet Dillinger couldn't shoot any better than that," and the cop agreed.

John even sang when we rode the roller coaster. He sang, then he leaned over and kissed me when we went around the curves. He never rode the roller coaster once. He had to ride it at least three times, then he'd get off staggering, as if he were dizzy, and sing that goofy song again, "Hey, Hey, How Am I Doin'?"

"I'm serious," I say, studying the tavern. "Something's wrong."

John's supposed to meet his attorney at Gilardi's. Mr. Piquett's going to give him the name of a plastic surgeon.

I can see a young couple sitting at a table in the front window. There's a pitcher of beer on the table before them, and they're toasting each other with steins.

It's cold but sunny, another Monday afternoon. Not much different than any other. But I have this feeling.

"It looks all right to me," John says. "Everything seems to be kosher."

A woman wearing high heels walks by with a Pomeranian on a leash, and a fat man with a cigar for a mouth lurches out of Gilardi's.

"It looked all right in Tucson—to everyone but Mary— and look where you ended up. You should have listened to her."

"Yeah," John says, watching the street.

A skinny guy in a checked yellow suit bicycles by, and someone who could have been a prizefighter pushes an apple cart. His nose is broken and he's bent over, his huge hands gripping the cart.

"There goes a thousand rounds of defeat," John says.

"You take the car around the block a couple of times

while I go into the tavern and check it out," I say. "If things are all right, I'll come to the door and signal you. If things aren't, I probably won't be coming to the door and you can keep going."

"I don't like it."

"I don't either, not any of it," I say. "That's why I've got to go in first."

JOHN DILLINGER

I drive around the block three times, but Billie still isn't there. I'm afraid I'll attract too much attention if I drive by again, so I park the car around the corner from the tavern.

I buy an apple from the vendor with the ruined face. I give him a dollar, telling him to keep the change.

He says, "Jeez, tanks," and I can see the spaces where his teeth used to be.

Then I see five men with submachine guns and pistols coming out of Gilardi's and Billie's with them. They've cuffed her hands behind her back, but I can hear her shouting, "You let John get away, you fools! He was standing in a crowd near the door when you told me to put my hands up."

A heavyset man wearing a gray suit pushes her head down then he shoves her into the backseat of a black Buick parked at the curb. The five men get into the car, and I watch it move past us in the fading light.

"I wonder what the hell's goin' on?" the apple vendor asks, his voice lisping.

BILLIE FRECHETTE

"Look at me," Agent Purvis says. "Look me in the eye."

He puts his hand under my chin, trying to force me to

look up so they can shine the lights in my face. He's a little guy who speaks with a drawl.

"If you don't look up, I'll make you look up, Miss Frechette. I want you to tell me where Dillinger is."

"I'm not telling you anything."

I can feel the pressure of his hand under my chin.

My neck aches, I'm sweating from the hot lights, and my period's ready to start. I can feel it.

Purvis says, "I don't like to hit women, Miss Frechette."

He probably grew up in some shitty little town in the Carolinas and fucked pigs.

"I don't talk to pig fuckers," I say.

I can hear the men who are standing behind the lights laugh, then Purvis slaps me so hard my ears ring.

"I don't have to listen to your filthy mouth," he says.

LEMON MOATE

"It's kind of joke around here," Mr. Dillinger says. "You see, the Mooresville police don't really want to arrest John 'cause someone could get hurt. When the cops are comin', they turn their sirens on six miles down the road, so John will have time to hide. So he'll know they're comin'. People around here refer to the road out front as 'Dillinger Road,' even though that ain't its name. Everyone in Mooresville knows John's a good boy."

"A good boy?"

"Yes, sir. You can ask anyone around here."

I stop at the gas station and ask the attendant, "Do you know John Dillinger?"

"Don't you reporter fellows get tired of askin' the same questions? Everyone in Mooresville knows John."

"What do you think of him?"

"I like him fine."

The back of the attendant's hands are freckled, and there's grease under his nails. He stands next to a dirty sink, scrubbing his hands with Boraxo and water.

I'd hate a job like his.

"Could you tell me something about Dillinger's background?"

"You could have asked him yourself last weekend. He came in to get gas and have his oil changed."

"While every cop in the nation was looking for him?"

"Sure, John and his girlfriend was here for a family reunion. They hung around the station awhile, talkin' and laughin' and drinkin' Cokes, and John gave me a ten-dollar tip. Boy howdy," the attendant says. "It made me want to take up bank robbin'."

An old man sitting on a bench in front of Gaffey's Pool Hall tells me, "Tourists come to Mooresville to see where John used to hang out. For a while, I was selling envelopes that was supposed to contain photographs of John for fifty cents. It's a way to supplement my retirement. When people found out the envelopes was empty, I'd say, 'I guess he got away from you, too,' and laugh. Even the police thought it was a big joke."

The manager of the bank tells me, "I saw John on the street last weekend, he and his financée, Miss Frechette. John was visiting some old friends."

"You mean he can stroll around his hometown, eighteen miles from Indianapolis, without anybody turning him in?"

"Nobody ever did," the banker says.

Red and I walk up a steep hill near the house where he and his sister, Jenna, grew up. It's been snowing since we arrived but winter in the Upper Peninsula begins in early September and ends in late May or June.

Summer lasts a day.

Red says, "I lost my fingers in a sleighing accident near here. I was comin' down this hill when my sled turned over and the blades run over my hand."

Red takes his fur-lined glove off, as if he still can't believe the middle and index fingers are missing from his right hand, then he puts the glove on again.

The snow's still swirling around us, and our breath hangs in the air as we trudge toward the house. We can see smoke rising from the chimney. I wish we had snowshoes.

Some of Red's friends from the old days are coming over for a poker game later tonight, and Jenna's making hot dogs and sauerkraut. Red and I bought some Schlitz beer and saltwater taffy when we were in Sault Sainte Marie.

"Maybe we should have gone to Louisville, after all," Red says. We'd heard the cops were expecting us there, so we'd come north. "I forgot how cold it gets in the Soo."

"Forget about the cold," I say. "Harry and Charley and I went to Tucson because of the warm weather, and look what happened to us."

"Yeah."

Red stomps his feet in the hall between the front porch and the living room when we go into the house, and we hang our hats and coats on a rack made out of antlers.

"I told Jenna I was glad I was wounded comin' out of that bank in East Chicago, otherwise I'd be waitin' for the chair with Charley and Harry in Ohio," he says. "Funny, I wanted to catch the first bus out of here when I was a kid. But Jenna, she just wanted to get married, have kids, join the PTA and live in the house where we grew up and, damn it, that's just what she done."

I can smell the sauerkraut and hot dogs when we go through the double doors into the front room.

"I used to think she was crazy," Red continues, "but I'll be lucky to be alive this time next year, and she's the happiest person I know."

"Let's have one of those red hots," I say.

HOMER VAN METER

I tell Baby Face, "I didn't say I screwed her, for Christ sake, I said I knew her," but he never listens.

"It's the same thing," Baby Face says. "It's in the Bible. When it says somebody 'knew' somebody else, it meant they were doin' it. They were screwin', see? I learned all that shit from the nuns."

A fat guy wearing a knit cap looks our way, scowling because Nelson's voice is as irritating as a crying baby's and it carries.

Baby Face and I have been playing cribbage since we arrived at the lodge. I've lost count of how many games I've won, but I could retire at a dollar a point.

I hate the little runt, but John says he's valuable.

Sometimes I get tired of what John says.

I told Laurel I can only stand so much recreation, and nature gives me the willies. I'd rather ride the worst streetcar in Chicago than take a walk in the woods. All you've got out here is snow and pine trees and bear poop. Laurel says it isn't that bad, but it would be if she hadn't come with me.

Red's girl told us about the lodge, because she thought it would be a good place to get away from the heat. Pat went to college for a semester, but she likes to talk like a gun moll. Pretty soon she'll be smoking cigars, like Bonnie Parker, and writing bad poetry. Pat loves to use words like *gat* and *heat* and *G-man*.

"I think Pat used to go with this guy I knew in Chicago," Baby Face says. "He was always drinkin' champagne—he thought it made him special—and he'd pour it on a dame's twat. He had a face like a cunt-lapper."

"Why don't you shut up?" I ask. "I'm tired of you."

"Winnin' don't give you the right to talk to me like that," Baby Face says. "You'd better watch what you say."

John and the proprietor have been playing pinochle all afternoon while Mrs. Wanatka comes in and out of the bar, listening.

John told me, "You couldn't whisper your thoughts to your pillow without Mrs. Wanatka knowing all about it five minutes later."

Each time Wanatka wins a hand he says, "This is lucky day," but he's cheating.

I guess John hasn't said anything because he's glad to have company. Everyone at the lodge has a woman but John, and he isn't used to traveling alone.

Billie got two years for harboring a fugitive.

I can hear the cards slide across the felt tabletop as Wanatka deals.

He says, "When I come to America I only know one word of English, *sonofbeach,* but I'm quick learner. I work as roustabout for circus, as boxer, as bellboy, but I get tired of the bell go *ding ding* all the time when people want something, so I save money and become proprietor of Little Bohemia in Chicago. Gene Tunney even come there one time, and we talk about boxing, but Nan want our son, Emil, Jr., to grow up in the country so we come here, fifty mile from Rhinelander and thirteen mile from nowhere, and open new Little Bohemia."

John watches Wanatka spread his cards out on the green felt.

"*Sonofbeach,*" Wanatka says. "I win again."

"You'll see," Laurel says, "things will be all right," but John just nods.

I don't know what Laurel's doing with a guy like me. Sometimes I feel worn-out, but she can dance all night and sing and joke. Maybe I could, too, when I was twenty-one. I don't remember.

"Who was the first carpenter?" Laurel asks.

"I don't know." John shrugs. "Jesus?"

"No, it was Eve. She made Adam's banana stand."

Red and Baby Face laugh, but John just sits there, looking at the half-eaten steak on his plate.

"She made Adam's banana stand," Laurel says, her blond hair glistening. She was a brunette when we met, but she says blondes have more fun. "Don't you get it?"

"Yeah, it's a riot," John says.

"I realized I hated cops when I was in the fifth grade," I say.

Laurel's sitting next to me on the couch in front of the stone fireplace, her head resting on my shoulder. The light flickers on her face, and I can feel her body against mine.

Maybe I could get to like it here.

I tell her, "My parents had a small farm near Fort Wayne. There was a long dirt road that led down to our house from the main highway, and I saw a car coming down the road one night. There was a full moon. The car didn't have its lights on, but I could see it was from the sheriff's department. It stopped next to the cornfield and this deputy pulled something out of the backseat and dropped it there.

"The next morning my dad found the body of a Mexican. Somebody had worked him over with a blackjack. I told my dad what I'd seen and he told me to shut up about it, never to say anything.

"He called the sheriff and some deputies showed up later that day. One of them said, 'Somebody sure worked that spic over,' and the others laughed, then they took the body away and said they were going to launch a thorough investigation.

"Dad began to drink heavily, and he had what the doctors called 'a general nervous collapse' a year later. He'd had a good job as a railroad conductor, but he lost it.

"The dirty bastards not only killed that Mexican, they ruined my dad's life."

JOHN DILLINGER

"I'm glad Homer joined up with us," I say.

"Yeah, he's a right guy," Red says.

He and I are sitting at the bar with Pat. She's wearing a low-cut red dress that accentuates her breasts and her red hair and . . . Sometimes I'd run a comb through Billie's hair when we lay on the bed together.

"Remember when they threw Homer in the hole for tryin' to escape that time?" Red asks.

Sometimes. . . .

"They had to drag him there after the night captain worked him over. Then they beat him with blackjacks every night for two months. How the hell'd he stand it?"

"I guess you can get used to anything," I say, but I'm not sure.

I remember Homer was covered with bruises when they let him out of the hole. Any other guy would have been screaming and cursing, but Homer laughed and threw his back out of joint, hobbling around the yard like this guard who was hunchbacked.

Homer said, "The guard lisped when he got mad so it

sounded like he was spitting. He'd say, 'You tink you're a tough guy,' then he'd club me. I thought the bastard was going to throw his arm out of joint."

Homer kept bringing his arm down, hard, while he told the story, showing us how the guard had hit him. You could hear his bones crack.

It was awful, but we were all laughing.

Homer had the word *Hope* tattooed on his forearm because it was something you never wanted to lose, he said.

I keep telling myself that but, right now, it isn't working very well.

"Laurel told me this joke," Pat says. "Two worms were crawling down the road. One stopped . . . one crawled on."

"Then what happened?" Red asks.

"Ask John," Pat says.

"I know who you are," Wanatka says.

"Yeah?"

"I see gun in shoulder holster when you lean forward and we play cards. I tell wife I seen you before, and we find your photo in *Tribune*."

Emil leans against the bar, waiting for me to say something, but I just look at him.

He's short, stocky, and his plaid shirt's too tight. He's a long way from Bohemia, but you can tell he grew up poor. He's one of those guys who doesn't want to spend money on clothes. He keeps telling himself he's going to lose weight, that the pounds around his middle are temporary, but it's a losing battle. He might as well get in the ring with Max Baer.

"Paper say you weigh one hundred fifty pounds and you have small scar near lip and on back of left hand."

"It said all that, did it?"

"Yeah."

"Tell me something, Emil. You're not afraid are you?"

"I don't want no shooting match, no cops coming with guns and *bang bang*. Everything I got to my name is right here."

He walks across the room to the fireplace, his shoulders slumped.

"Why don't you do me big favor? You fellows leave in hurry."

"Emil, I'm tired. I want to sleep a few days. Rest up."

I stand next to him, putting a hand on his shoulder. I can feel his tension.

"I'll pay you well, then we'll get out."

"You tell the missus that," he says.

"Don't worry, I'll take care of everything."

We have bacon and eggs for breakfast, and Mrs. Wanatka serves us dark coffee in ceramic mugs.

"Coffee is European-roasted, like Old Country," Wanatka says, but I can't tell the difference.

The temperature's just above freezing, but Red says, "You can't stay inside forever, waitin' for good weather, when you live here. I'm goin' out for some target practice. How 'bout the rest of you?"

Wanatka says, "I have twenty-two target pistol."

"You might as well have a cap gun," Red says, then he goes upstairs to get a rifle.

Emil, Jr. lines up some tin cans against a snowbank about three hundred feet in front of us. He's wearing a beanie and a red muffler, and he's probably nine.

Baby Face fires first, but he keeps missing, the bullets plowing into the snow.

Red and Homer are laughing, and Wanatka laughs with them.

Baby Face hands Red the rifle and asks Wanatka, "What's so fuckin' funny?"

"I think badman like you be a better shot," Wanatka says.

"Maybe I ought to get the Thompson. Maybe I could improve the looks of this dump if I fired a few rounds into the side of the building."

"Forget it," I say.

The lodge is about five hundred yards from Highway 51, but people around here are hunters. They'd know the difference between a rifle and a submachine gun, and we don't want to attract any more attention than we have to. We're just some businessmen up here for a vacation. That's what Wanatka's supposed to tell anyone who comes to the lodge for a drink or dinner.

"Yeah, I guess it ain't such a good idea," Baby Face says.

He and the kid play catch, but Baby Face throws the ball harder and harder.

Wanatka doesn't notice because he and Homer are firing the rifle, shooting it out with each other.

The white sky glares through the holes in the cans as they bounce into the air.

Emil, Jr. drops the ball, rubbing his hands together.

"What are you, a pussy?" Baby Face asks.

"Let the kid alone," I say. "It isn't his fault you're a lousy shot."

"What're you talkin' about? The kid and I are just havin' some fun, ain't we, kid?" But Emil, Jr. is crying.

A drunk from the CCC camp down the road sits next to Red and Pat at the bar.

A woman is singing a sad song about love on the radio, so I turn the dial to another station.

The drunk says, "Hey, I like that song."

He's blond, and he sounds like he just got off the boat from Sweden. I expect him to say *by jimminy*.

174

"Don't mind my buddy," Red says. "He has a broken heart and he can't listen to nothin' like that."

"Yah, I had a broken heart once. I go to whorehouse in Mercer every Saturday night for month. Then I met Lulu."

Pat laughs. "I can tell you're a sensitive guy."

"Yah, that's me," the drunk says. "Sensitive."

He tries to light a cigarette, but the matches keep going out. Finally, Red lights it for him.

"Thanks," the drunk says. "Let me buy you drink."

"I've already had one," Red says. "I'm not much of a drinker."

"You have one with me, by golly, or I pour drink down your throat. You think you're too good to have drink with Sven?"

Red tells the barkeep, "This man is pretty tough, and he's not goin' to take no for an answer. You'd better give me a small beer."

"I knew this guy who used to eat off the floor," Red says.

He and Pat and I are the only ones left in the bar. I think they're afraid to leave me alone.

"What was his name?" Pat asks. "Billy Goat?"

"Nah. It was Vinnie Lynd. He was one of them guys who wouldn't eat meat or chicken. He wouldn't even eat cheese."

"He must have been a vegetarian," Pat says.

"A what?"

"Vegan. They live on fruits and nuts."

"Yeah, he was nuts all right. He was a skinny, pale-lookin' guy who didn't have no hair. I think it fell out 'cause he didn't eat sensible."

"I don't think that would make your hair fall out," Pat says.

"We was havin' dinner one night when he drops a piece of cauliflower on the floor. I don't pay much attention, but Vinnie picks it up and heads for the john. I figure he's gonna throw it away, but he says he washed it off in the john and ate it."

"Why would he tell you that?" I ask.

"He was a crazy fucker."

"I can't imagine what kind of childhood he must have had," Pat says. "That's disgusting."

Red pours the last of his beer into a glass and says, "I'll tell you disgusting. I'm at the Phoenix Theatre in Chicago one night, listenin' to this band. The guy who's singin' is naked, but he don't act like it. He's movin' around the stage while the bass player is plunkin' away, then someone from backstage comes out and gives the guy a chicken."

"I think we'd better go to bed," Pat says.

"It's flappin' its wings and cluckin', but the guy twists its head off, throwin' it into the audience. I swear to God, I think it clucked a time or two while it was flyin' through the air. Feathers are all over the joint and chicken blood is runnin' down the guy's leg, but he sticks his cock in the chicken. I never seen anything like it. There he is singin' along with his dick in this headless chicken."

"Some people will fuck anything," I say.

GEORGE NELSON

I follow Mrs. Wanatka's Chevy into Manitowish.

I told John he shouldn't have let her and the kid go, but her nephew's having a birthday party.

There'll be ice cream and noisemakers, and the kids will play pin the tail on the donkey.

John said, "I let Emil cheat me at pinochle, and I just gave him five hundred dollars. Why should he or Nan tell anyone we're here, especially when we're leaving in a few hours? Let the kid go to the party."

"I don't trust Mrs. Wanatka," I said.

176

She referred to me as 'Baby Face,' and I told her to shut her yap.

"Look," I said, "I don't like dames with a smart mouth. It would be a shame if you got hurt."

The woods along the road are deep and dark.

Mrs. Wanatka turns her lights on, the rear end of the Chevy sliding on the black ice. It's dusk, and great flakes of snow come down like wounded butterflies.

Mrs. Wanatka parks in front of Nissen's General Store, and she and the kid go inside.

I park beside the Chevy, watching her. She bulges in all the wrong places.

She's talking to the grocer when I go up to the window. I rap on the glass and point a finger at her when she looks in my direction. The grocer's wearing a green eyeshade, and he puts her purchases into a paper sack. They smile at each other while the kid fidgets. He reminds me of the cretins I knew in the convent.

I'm standing there, waiting, when she and Emil, Jr. leave the store. A little bell tings as the door shuts behind them.

"What'd you buy?"

"Rock candy, some ice cream, party favors."

"Ain't it cold for ice cream?"

"Not when you're a kid."

Someone wearing a white smock puts a CLOSED sign in the window of the Dawn Patrol Barbershop across the street. He was probably in the war, and never got over it. That's what wrong with a lot of people. They never get over things.

"You're not going to do anything stupid, are you?"

"No. Of course not."

She hesitates a moment, as if she's going to say something else, but she and the kid just get into the Chevy.

I follow them down the road to her brother's place. I watch her turn into the driveway, then she and the kid go up the

porch steps in the snow. The venetian blinds are open, and I can
see a roomful of kids. Some of them are wearing pointed hats,
and the light's soft and yellow and friendly.

I sit in the car, watching them, until someone shuts the
blinds.

I never had a party when I was a kid.

They sang to me in the orphanage: "You've got the cutest little
baby face."

I didn't, I told them.

I ran down the halls, my fists bruised, my nose bloody.

I hold Helen close to me, my chin resting on her shoulder, my
hands on her breasts. My penis touches her buttocks, and I've
never wanted her more.

"Turn over."

When she does, I can see her large, dark eyes, even in
the dim light. She's small and pale and I knew I was going to
marry her the first time I watched her walk across the schoolyard
at Harrison High. It was late afternoon and she seemed to evap-
orate in the twilight.

"It's all right," she says.

I lie beside her, feeling foolish. Stupid.

I hate it when things go wrong.

"You're just tired."

"Yeah, that must be it. I'm tired."

MELVIN PURVIS

I can see the lights coming from the lodge as we approach it.
They seem phosphorescent in the darkness.

"These goddamn vests weigh a ton," one of my agents
says. "Mine's breaking my back."

"So? You can always go to a chiropractor later," I say. "At least you'll be alive."

I get tired of their complaining, but they've been whining since we flew into Rhinelander. "The last good-looking woman in this town left thirty years ago." "Hell, you can't blame her for that. I don't even think they have flush toilets here." Whining.

Two of the five cars we rented broke down on the way to Mercer, and eight agents ended up on the running boards. I could hear the two on my side cursing through the window.

"Why the hell would Dillinger hide out in a shithole like this?"

"Damned if I know."

"If I were him, I'd be sipping tequila in a hot pillow joint along the Mexican border. I'd have a senorita on each knee, and they'd have titties like cannonballs."

My men were holding rifles and shotguns, and their faces looked purple in the frozen moonlight as they hunched over. They could have been a species from another planet. Or aborigines.

"I'm going to tell Hoover he's an asshole when I turn in my resignation. You don't see him out here."

"Of course not. He's prancing around someplace in D.C., but he'll be the one who gets his picture in the paper."

Snow swirled in the headlights, and rocks from the country road pinged beneath the car. I could really feel the cold when I rolled my window down.

I said, "Why don't you men shut up? Just shut the hell up. We're almost there now."

HOMER VAN METER

Two guys from the CCC camp come into the bar. They're wearing denim overalls, but their mackinaws are different. One's yellow and one's blue.

179

"If I never see another fuckin' tree it'll be too soon," Blue says.

I can't imagine what it's like to work as a logger. It doesn't even have a good sound. Logger. Lunger.

I tell Laurel, "Some guys will do anything for a living."

"The Depression ruined people," she says. "The Depression and Roosevelt. Work used to mean something, but he took that away when he created all those dumb jobs. Nobody in his right mind would chop trees all day."

"You got that right, lady," Yellow says, and Blue laughs, coughing.

Laurel says, "We used to be a proud people."

"Well, not everyone can rob banks," I say.

Blue and Yellow look around the bar, drinking their beers.

John's playing a slot machine in the back corner. I can hear him pulling the handle each time he drops a quarter into the slot. There isn't much else to do in a place like this.

"Hell," Yellow says, rattling the dice in a leather cup. "Hell."

"I spent the night in a bus station in Wahoo, Nebraska once and had more fun than this," Blue says.

They finish their beers, waving at us when they walk by our table. I can hear a dog bark before the door shuts behind them.

Then John drops another quarter into the slot machine.

"My mother told me only pigs do it when they have their periods," Laurel says.

"It's what parents do. They're supposed to tell you all sorts of dumb crap. It must be in a book someplace."

"She never did a sensible thing in her life, but she thought she was special because she was a good Christian woman."

"You can't worry about stuff like that. It doesn't mean anything."

"You know what I finally told her?"

I shrug.

"'Oink,' I said. 'Oink, oink'"

MELVIN PURVIS

Two men come out of the bar and walk unsteadily across the snow to their car. This should be easy.

"The tall guy in the yellow mackinaw's Van Meter," I say. "The other's got to be Dillinger."

"You sure?"

"Of course I'm sure. Who else would it be?"

Their shadows stain the snow yellow in the moonlight. It looks like some big cat came by and pissed there.

"What'll we do?" Clegg asks, rubbing his hands together. His teeth chatter from the cold. Maybe he needs to take a piss.

"Tell them to surrender."

"Now?"

"Yeah."

"What do I say?"

They're getting into the car now. Dillinger's on the driver's side.

"How about 'Come out with your hands up or we'll fire?'"

Dillinger's started the car and one of them has turned the radio on. I'm standing here freezing and some fool is singing a song about love.

"Come out with your hands up or we'll fire!" Clegg yells.

Dillinger's backing up now.

"I don't think they heard me."

"Of course they heard you. They're escaping." I yell, "Fire! Fire!"

181

A dozen agents open up with rifles and submachine guns, and I watch the bullets hitting the car. They make a strange pocking sound, and the car looks like a piece of scrap metal in less than a minute. There are pieces of shattered glass where the windshield used to be, and I can see Dillinger slumped over the wheel.

The horn's blaring and the radio's still playing and steam's coming from the radiator. All four tires are flat, but the engine's still running. The car shudders, but someone's singing "All I Do Is Dream of You." The person who invented car radios was a fool.

Van Meter gets out on the passenger's side. He stands there swaying, clutching a bottle, then he sits down like a broken puppet.

I run over to the car, opening the door, and look at the driver. There are shards of glass embedded in his cheeks. He reminds me of a porcupine I shot when I was a kid. It was nothing but blood and needles.

"I never saw this guy before," I say. "Who the hell is he?"

Clegg's leaning over the man in the yellow mackinaw.

"How should I know? This guy says his name's John Morris. He's a cook at the CCC camp, and he's shot all to hell."

"Shit," I say. "Shit."

JOHN DILLINGER

We can hear machine guns firing when we go out the rear window onto a porch facing a lake.

We're all armed.

Homer says, "I always hated heights," but he jumps into a snowbank below the porch, and Red and I follow him, diving into the darkness. Then the three of us make our way along the icy shore. We can see the lights in a house owned by an old couple named Mitchell across the lake.

Mitchell's wife is sitting on the worn couch when we go into the house. There's a blue-and-gold comforter on her lap.

Red cuts the phone line with a pocketknife while Homer looks out the window. Waiting. Watching.

There's a picture of an Indian in a canoe and a poster for a Tom Mix movie, *Terror Trail,* above the couch. I'm an authority on terror, even if I don't know much about horses. I could have been Tom's technical advisor. I know all I need to about guns.

We can still hear the Thompsons firing across the lake.

I say, "You probably heard stories about me, but I'm not as bad as they claim. We're not going to hurt anyone. All we need is a ride to St. Paul."

"My wife's getting over the flu," Mitchell says. He's a soft-spoken old guy with gray hair. He could be my father.

Times must be hard. There's a sign on the porch—ROOMS FOR RENT—but the people who come to Star Lake all stay at the Lodge.

"We just want to borrow the car in the driveway," I say. "You won't tell on us, will you?"

I give Mitchell a hundred-dollar bill.

"I don't know a thing," he says.

MELVIN PURVIS

"Goddamn, you shoot place all to hell," Emil says. "You let bad guys get away and kill customer."

His wife sits at the bar, drinking whiskey and taking aspirin. She probably lives on jumbo and mulligan stew, and has a brain like mush. She has to hold the glass with both hands because she's shaking so badly. I hate peasants.

"How do you spell your last name, Emil?"

"W-a-n . . . Who care how name is spelled?"

"I need it for my report."

"One Polack's name is like another," Clegg says.

"I no Polack," Emil says.

"Yeah, right."

"W-a-n-a-t-k-a."

I write it in a spiral notebook.

"And how do you spell the town where Mrs. Wanatka's brother lives?"

"Who care how you spell town?"

"Just answer the question, Emil."

"Bad guys getting away while we have spelling bee."

"Don't get funny with us," Clegg says.

"You throw tear gas into building so wife and I come out with gangster women. We all crying. You tell us, 'Hands up' and we stand there in cold and answer stupid questions. Now more stupid questions."

"Just tell us how you spell the town, Emil."

"M-a-n-i-t-o . . . wish. Like 'wish you leave now.'"

"You and your wife were the ones who told us Dillinger was here."

"Yeah, that mistake all right. Mr. Dillinger give me five hundred dollars and treat me fine, but Nan say we have duty to be citizen and report him. Then you shoot big goddamn holes in lodge."

"I'd appreciate it if you didn't take the Lord's name in vain."

"Bullshit," Emil says.

GEORGE NELSON

It's late afternoon when I come to a cabin near Stearns Lake. An Indian in his late sixties is building a fire in front of the place, the smoke curling into the gray sky like the ashes of the dead.

The air smells like maple syrup.

I've been lost since I left the lodge, but I know there's an Indian reservation near Lac du Flambeau.

I tell the old man, "You'd better put the fire out."

"I don't put out no fire."

"You'll burn up the woods."

"Indians don't burn up no woods."

A woman and two girls come to the doorway of the cabin.

"Do you know who I am?" I ask.

They have long dark hair and large eyes, and their faces could be painted-on plates.

"I'm George Nelson."

The old Indian says, "You can help me tend the fire, George Nelson. There's a lot of work to do."

MAGGIE MANY MOONS

I give the man who calls himself George Nelson some bacon and fried eggs, give him some fresh bread and coffee.

He gives me two dollars, putting the bills on the table, then he gives my oldest, Dorothy, a dollar.

When he finishes dinner he asks, "Would you mind if I lay down a while? I've been walking a long ways."

There's a cot next to the wall.

I keep the girls out of the room, quiet, but I can tell George Nelson doesn't really sleep.

185

When he gets up he asks if we have a radio or a tele-phone—the things white men think they need.

"No," I tell him, "we could be killed, and no one would know anything about it."

"Don't you get the papers?"

"No."

He asks many questions, George Nelson does.

"Do you have any old clothes?"

"All we have is old clothes. We're Indians."

I give him a pair of Uncle Ollie's khaki-colored pants and a plaid jacket with the sleeves cut off, and George Nelson puts them on over his good clothes.

My five-year-old stands next to the cot where he slept with his eyes open.

Gertrude says, "Mommy, you should see the guns he has under his pillow."

JOHN DILLINGER

It must be late afternoon when we awaken.

We can hear shots in the distance, then a bullet shatters the back window of our car and someone says, "I'm hit."

Red slumps forward, reaching out, grabbing the empty air. There's blood on the car seat and a hole the size of a silver dollar where a bullet entered his back.

We'd been driving all night and most of the day when I pulled the car off a country road into some woods near North-field. We'd stopped for gas and Cokes at a small service station where I bought a newspaper.

"Listen to this," I said, reading Will Rogers's column. "'Well, the FBI had Dillinger surrounded and was all ready to shoot him when he come out of the lodge, but two other fellows come out first, so the FBI shot them instead.'"

I drive across a small bridge while Homer fires at the cops. They're using high-powered rifles, and they must be a quarter of a mile behind us.

Maybe the guy at the service station thought we looked suspicious. Maybe he had a nickel and called the cops when he thought I laughed too loudly at Will Rogers's story.

When you're in the city, you can count on some cop taking a bribe, but you never know what a small-town cop will do.

"I think the James Gang got shot-up near here," Homer says.

"The hell with the James Gang," Red says. "Just get me to a doctor."

GEORGE NELSON

"I've got to get to Eagle River and see whether my friends made it there or not," I say.

I don't think Maggie believes me, but she makes the sandwiches I asked for, nodding. She slices the bread, her knife gleaming in the afternoon light, and I can almost taste the ham and cheese. The kitchen's pungent with peppers and salami.

Maggie told me she'd been raised Catholic and wondered why I was surprised. I suppose I thought she'd be a heathen, praying before idols, but I didn't want to tell her that.

I say, "You're not as dumb as you pretend to be."

Maggie smiles, putting the sandwiches into a brown-paper bag with some maple-sugar cakes. The sap's running real good, and the Indians boil it in large barrels at the sugar camp.

I give Maggie twenty dollars, "For making my lunch," and another fifty, "For being kind."

Maggie shakes my hand solemnly, "Thank you, George Nelson," then Ollie and I start up the dirt road leading to the highway. I wonder if anyone but me got away alive.

It's almost dark by the time we reach the highway because Ollie can't walk very fast.

He says, "My legs hurt from the rheumatism, George Nelson."

Some men are fishing alongside a little lake. Ollie and I watch them awhile. They're catching minnows and bottom feeders, and I tell Ollie, "Let's go fishing, too."

Someone lights a lantern and someone else leans over a small fire holding a frying pan, singing a Stephen Foster song, and I can smell the fish cooking. I should have been born in a place like this.

Two men are getting out of an old Packard next to the lake holding their poles.

"Which one of you owns the car?" I ask.

The guy on the driver's side nods, setting a tackle box on the hood.

"I'll give you five hundred—cash—for the keys to it and the title."

"It ain't worth that much, mister."

"It is to me."

"Well, then, I sure wish I had the title with me. It's home somewhere," he says, but it comes out "*some ere.*"

"I'll take it without the title."

When I hand him five one-hundred dollar bills, he just stares at them. I don't think he's seen that much money before.

I say, "I know you're going to report this, but give me a little time, all right?"

"Hell, yes," he says. "We've got some fish to catch."

A freckle-faced attendant fills the car with gas when Ollie and I stop at a service station. I give the attendant ten dollars, telling him to keep the change, after he checks the oil. He can't be much older than sixteen, and he whistles.

"Mister, you must rob banks to tip like that."

"Sure, kid."

I let Ollie out, giving him seventy-five dollars, half-a-mile off the main highway. It's cold and dark and he looks small standing there with a wool scarf wrapped around his neck and a gray stocking cap jammed onto his head.

"Will you be all right?" I ask.

He nods, stuffing the money into his coat pocket. "You take care of yourself, George Nelson. Don't shoot no more cops."

JOHN DILLINGER

"I'm dying," Red says, and it becomes a refrain—a death chant. He's dying as we head south along the east bank of the Mississippi River, dying when we exchange cars with a young couple named Francis near La Crosse, dying when we stop to get him some soda at a small grocery in northern Illinois, dying when we stop for dinner at the Seafood Inn—miles from any sea—in Elmhurst.

It's a mob hangout, and there's a doctor there we can trust; but he tells us what we already know, "It's hopeless," and Red dies Friday night, out of his pain at last. He always liked weekends.

Homer and I dig a deep grave for Red in the sand dunes near Burns Harbor, Indiana. It isn't far from where we met, serving time together. The sand's blowing in the wind coming off Lake Michigan, and it's a clear night. The stars could be candles in the sky.

I remember Red thought there was something going on between Little Orphan Annie and Daddy Warbucks, remember how he liked to tease Makley about the stripper with the snake, and I remember the time the guards at Michigan City beat him for skipping rope. I remember him being wounded when he came out of the First National Bank, remember him saying he didn't think he'd live another year when we were at his sister's, less than a month ago.

Red was a hard-luck guy.

When we put him into the grave, we pour four cans of lye onto his face and hands so no one will be able to identify him.

Homer says, "I hate to do this, Red, but I know you'd do the same for me," then we cover the body with sand.

MELVIN PURVIS

"Dillinger's ruining my life," I say. Walking along the beach. With my wife. Under a jagged sky. The clouds seem broken. As if someone forced the wrong pieces of a puzzle together. It's a gray day. And night isn't far away.

Rosanne says, "He's ruining mine, too. You never have time. For me. Now."

The waves wither. On the sand.

"It's terrible," Rosanne says, "but I actually pray. For the man's death."

At night. I wither when she touches me. I can still see. The man staggering. Out of the car. Holding a bottle. Frozen in the headlights. Dying. It is all the dream. Of an insomniac.

Rosanne says, "Get down on your knees with me."

There are no shadows. In the gray light.

My knees sink. Into the moist sand.

"Dear God," Rosanne says. Trying to pray. "Dear God."

"Help us," I say.

"I know it's wrong," Rosanne says, "to ask for the death of another man, Lord, but I'm asking for it. I'm asking for the death of John Dillinger because he's . . ."

"Evil," I say.

"He's evil, Lord."

We hold hands. On the beach. Our voices. Carried away by the wind. There's a lighthouse. On the cape. Somewhere. Its light flashing. Like Morse code. Being sent. By an insane person.

"Amen," I say. Kneeling. Under the broken sky.

SUMMER 1934

John stands outside the Blue Bird Café, making faces through the window. He knows my shift ends in a few minutes.

The waitress who's come on duty watches him, laughing. "Who's the guy in the gray suit?"

"Someone I met at the Barrel of Fun last night."

"What's his name?"

"Jimmy. Jimmy Lawrence."

"He kind of looks like Dillinger to me."

"Nah, Dillinger's a lot cuter," I say.

JOHN DILLINGER

It's good to be with a woman again.

I bring Polly home to Indiana, and we stay at a small hotel outside Greenfield. There's a sign at the edge of town saying James Whitcomb Riley grew up here.

I tell the night clerk, "I never heard of Riley."

The clerk watches me, bored, as I sign the register.

"Riley wrote a poem titled 'The Two Holer.' He was a big deal around here forty, fifty years ago, but nobody gives a shit about Hoosier life half a century ago," the clerk says, smiling. You can tell he's pleased with himself. "All people want to talk about these days is Dillinger."

"I can see why," Polly says. "Who'd want to read a poem about an outhouse?"

It's good to have a woman again.

We lie on the bed, smoking, talking quietly, after we've made love.

Polly rearranged our pillows because she wanted the open ends of the cases to face each other, "So the love won't leak out. If you watch the little things, the big things take care of themselves," she said.

She's twenty-six and was married to a cop in Gary.

Her breasts glisten when she gets up to wash her stockings. There's a small sink next to the window with the big moon. Everything's black and white, except for Polly's red hair.

She says, "I was in an accident a few years ago and my legs still bother me in humid weather."

When she comes back to bed, we make love again, then fall asleep on top of the sheets.

I can hear thunder in the distance when I awaken. I stand at the open window a long time, watching the sky crack, then I go over to the sink to get a glass of water.

Polly's stockings are still there, but I don't mind.

I'm holding Polly when she awakens in the middle of the night.

"I wish your last name was different," I say.

"Why?"

"I had a buddy named Hamilton. It took him a long time to die, and it hurt a lot."

"I'm sorry."

"Yeah, you would have liked Red," I say. "Almost everyone did."

We go to see my father at the farm.

He tells Polly, "I thought you and Johnnie would be married by now."

"This is Polly, Dad. Polly." Sometimes I think I don't want to get old, but I probably don't have to worry. "Billie . . . went away."

"Yes," he says, but his eyes are blank.

Audrey leads him into the kitchen, a hand on his shoulder.

She speaks quietly. "You can help me prepare dinner, Dad."

She'll have him shred the lettuce and peel cucumbers, his huge hands shaking, then he'll dice tomatoes and cut up radishes while she makes a vinaigrette dressing. She'll watch him, worried he'll cut himself, and remember how he used to swing a scythe for hours when he was in the field. The forlorn rags of growing old.

There'll be green onions because Audrey knows I like them, and an avocado and more. Strawberries and ice cream for dessert.

Sometimes I think about leaving for California—or Mexico. But there's never enough money, one more job to pull, something.

I don't want to leave home.

I can smell frog legs, sizzling in olive oil, smell the baking-powder biscuits in the oven. After dinner, Audrey and I will do the dishes. It's always been our special time. She was the mother I never knew when I was five. I had to stand on a stool to help her.

Polly and I go out onto the back porch. I show her the pocket watch my father gave me. The initials *JD* are engraved in script on the tarnished silver case.

"Dad said, 'You and I know time,' but I don't know what he was talking about. I don't think he did, either. Then he gave me this. It's broken."

"A lot of things are," Polly says.

"He's usually . . . better than this."

"It's all right, John. He's a nice man. Kind."

"Yeah."

We stand there a long time, silently, holding hands, watching the sky blaze.

"You don't know what it's like," Polly says, "being a waitress. People think you're stupid, that you'd amount to something if you had any sense, any initiative. They don't even see you unless they're looking for your reflection in an empty coffee cup. It's like being invisible."

"You look fine to me," I say, then Audrey calls, "Dinner's ready," and Polly and I go back into the kitchen.

I remember: I put my arms around my stepmother while the music box I'd bought her played "Waltzing Matilda." I was nine and "Mom" was teaching me how to dance.

The room seems smaller now. I don't know what happened to the music box, but Mom's gone.

So many things are lost: the friends of my youth, the coal trains rumbling by at dawn.

We'd gather the coal that fell beside the tracks, digging the black chunks out of the snow. We'd sell them to the women with large dark eyes who spoke with accents and wore babushkas and whose homes were always filled with crying children.

Mom sang, "Waltzing Matilda," as we two-stepped our way across the hardwood floor. She counted, "One, two, three," keeping time with the music as we dipped and bowed and the curtains blew in the soft wind, my small arms around her ample waist.

Mom smelled like crushed apples because she'd been in the orchard all afternoon. I could feel her strength as I held her, dancing. I knew she was never going to grow old or die, the way my mother had. This Mom was never going to leave me.

Dipping and bowing in the soft light, she counted, "One, two, three," singing our song.

We danced.

"I think the guy who runs this joint is a fairy," Baby Face says. "He calls himself Michael Angelo, for Christ sake, and he sang countertenor in the opera."

"There aren't any countertenors since they stopped castrating people," I say. "Their voices aren't high enough."

The guy Nelson's talking about manages the Green Mill. He's leaning against the bar across the room, talking to some funny man named Joe E. Lewis who works here.

"So what if he's a fairy?" John says. "Do you have something against fairies?"

"Yeah, they're always flutterin' around," Baby Face says. "They make me nervous."

"Everyone makes you nervous," I say, "cops, fairies, countertenors."

"Nobody makes me as nervous as cops," Baby Face says, "not even fairies."

"The three of us could take this train I've been watching," John says. "It's a mail train, but it carries a lot of cash. All we need is a little nitro to blow the door off the mail car."

"We ought to stay with what we know best, if you ask me," Baby Face says, "stick to robbin' banks."

"Who's asking you?" I say.

"We'd have enough money to last us the rest of our lives. We could go to Mexico—or somewhere."

"I went to Mexico once," Baby Face says, "and I ain't never goin' there again. I had the shits the whole time, and I didn't even drink the water. Didn't drink nothin'. You go to some of the villages and they don't even have flush toilets, for Christ sake, but they got bugs we ain't even discovered yet. The hell with Mexico, John. Stay away from there."

———

"There's this bank in South Bend," Baby Face says. "It's a beauty. The three of us could be in and out in five minutes, easy as pie."

"Yeah, everything's easy as pie till someone starts shooting," I say. "Look what happened at Little Bohemia."

"We got away, didn't we?"

"Tell that to Red," John says.

"They tried to kill me, tried to run me over, but I yanked the fuckin' car door open and started firing," Baby Face says. "I hit one cop over the right eye and shot the other through the throat, but the sonofabitch got out of the car and started running. I could see the blood spurting out of his neck in the headlights. Everyone thought he was going to die, but he was too dumb, I guess." Baby Face laughs. "The fool made it, but I'll bet he has one hell of a sore throat."

"I'll bet he does," John says.

POLLY HAMILTON

"They want to deport me for running brothel," Anna says. She's a husky, square-faced woman who speaks with an accent.

She rented me a room when she shut down the whorehouse. There's a CLOSED sign hanging on the front door, but men still knock on it in the middle of the night.

John brought us to the Greek's for strawberry sundaes.

We sit next to the window at a wrought-iron table while Gus Gianopulus stands behind the counter, smiling. All of his ice cream is homemade, and it comes in thirteen flavors.

John always orders strawberry, but Gus always asks, "What flavor you have today? Vanilla, chocolate, chocolate chip?"

Gus has a singsong voice and speaks with an accent. "Banana, orange sherbet, strawberry?"

Sometimes I think everyone in Chicago speaks with an accent.

"Sundae used to be spell like day of week, but Christians say it a sacrilege so spelling change," Gus says. "How you like that?"

"They're probably the same people who put Anna out of business," John says, and Anna agrees.

"Same men who come to my house for good time want me to leave country now, want to send me back to Romania. They call me 'undesirable alien.'"

John wipes some ice cream from his chin with a napkin. When he does, I can see the shoulder holster and the butt of the .45 under his seersucker jacket.

"It can be a cruel world, Anna."

"Two time I'm arrested for running disorderly house in Gary and two time Governor Leslie pardon me. Now Governor McNutt want Immigration Department to get rid of me."

"Maybe you should have opened an ice cream parlor," John says.

We can see the steam rising from the street when we leave the Biograph Theatre. It's raining and the humidity's stifling.

I tell John, "It's like trying to breathe through a wet cloth." The lights from the marquee glisten on the pavement, and cars seem to slide by, skidding around corners.

I've never known anyone who loves the movies as much as John. I hold on to his arm in the rainy darkness.

He took me to see Wallace Beery and Fay Wray in *Viva Villa,* and he's quiet, thoughtful, when the film ends.

Beery, as Villa, kept crisscrossing Mexico, searching for *Federales* to kill. He forced Wray to go with him, and she looked as scared as she did in that movie about the ape.

John's . . . searching. He wouldn't have to force me to go with him.

He says, "I'll be thirty-one next week."

He stops in front of the Biograph Barbershop. The barber must have gone hours ago, but there's a night light burning in the back room.

John's thinking about moving to someplace in California named Petaluma and raising chickens. "People call it 'the egg basket of the world,'" he says. "Maybe we could lose ourselves there." He lights a cigarette, studying his reflection in the rainy window. "I don't know what I want to do the rest of my life, but I can't go on robbing banks forever."

JOHN DILLINGER

"I love it," Baby Face says. "The citizens of Mercer County want to get rid of Purvis. They sent a petition to the Justice Department asking for his dismissal, 'at least until Dillinger is caught or killed,' because of the way he and his agents fucked up at Little Bohemia."

"Does it really say they 'fucked up' in the paper?" I ask.

He's reading from the *Tribune* while we wait for the results of a race he bet on; there's a bookmaking parlor in the loft above the Biograph.

"I wonder how come you get all the press?" Baby Face asks. His skin's blotchy from the heat.

"I guess I'm just a colorful guy."

"Yeah."

I can see the marquee from a small window in front of the loft. W. C. Fields is starring in *You're Telling Me*. I saw him in *The Fatal Glass of Beer* and thought he looked like someone who'd hit bottom but didn't pity himself. You can learn a lot from movies.

"The citizens are pissed because the raid was carried out in such a stupid manner as to bring about the deaths of two men and injury to four others," Baby Face says. "And none of the dead or injured were gangsters."

"Everyone keeps forgetting about Red," I say.

POLLY HAMILTON

"It's a hell of a note," John says, "being made Public Enemy Number One on my thirty-first birthday."

John sent me two-dozen roses and an amethyst ring, addressed to Cleopatra, before he picked me up in the taxi that brought us to the French Casino.

I didn't know there were so many taxis in Chicago. I think we must have taken them all, swirling through the hot, steaming streets. John Dillinger and Cleopatra, leaning against each other, laughing, when the drivers corner too quickly. John loves riding in taxis, seeing things, even if he doesn't know where he's going. "See," he'll say, "see," pointing at a cloud, a lake, a billboard. The guy I married never took me any place.

I say, "Hoover's a pissant, a little pissant. At least he could have waited until tomorrow instead of trying to spoil your birthday."

A waiter wearing a tuxedo pours champagne into our glasses.

"Tomorrow's *your* birthday."

"Yeah, but Hoover doesn't know that."

I'll be twenty-seven.

"I still think the bastard could have waited till the day after tomorrow," John says. "Some people just don't have any consideration for others."

"I don't trust the cunt," Baby Face says. "She thinks she's got a glass ass or somethin'. When she was in Gary, she worked out of the Kostur Hotel, and called herself Katie from the Kostur, like it was a special kingdom or somethin'. Some guys I know said she was a lousy lay."

"Anna's all right," I say, then the barber puts a hot towel over my face. There's no law against being a lousy lay.

"No, she ain't. She's always whinin'. Complainin' about bein' shipped back to Romania."

Baby Face is sitting in the chair next to mine at the Biograph Barbershop.

It's hard to talk with a towel over your face.

"I wouldn't want to go to Romania, either. Would you?"

"That's got nothin' to do with it, John. It's all the pissin' and moanin' she does."

Maybe Baby Face talks so tough because he's such a little guy.

When we leave the barbershop, his face red from the hot towels, he's almost strutting. He tugs at the brim of his cap, his eyes narrowing. I think he'd like to walk down the street with a machine gun under his arm.

"No one told her she had to run a whorehouse," Baby Face says. "People who are always whinin' make me nervous."

"Everyone makes you nervous," I say. "Cops, fairies, countertenors, hookers from Romania. We already established that."

"Yeah, well, I still don't like it," Baby Face says.

"Baby Face doesn't trust Anna," I say.

Polly leans into me as we dance, and I can feel her

breasts, smell the lavender and myrrh in her hair. There's smoke and jasmine and frankincense in the air.

"Anna's all right," Polly says. "She's just worried about her son. Steve's twenty-three, he was born here, he isn't going to Romania." Her words run together. "Maybe she'd never see him again."

I love to samba.

"That's what I told Baby Face," I say. "Anna's all right."

Polly's wearing a low-cut red dress that accentuates her hair, and I can see the dark cleft between her breasts.

I bought her a white Chevrolet convertible for her birthday and filled the backseat with roses and champagne.

"Polly, hold me," I say, but I'm thinking of Billie.

We awaken in a small town I don't know the name of in Missouri, then we make love.

I can hear a wolf howling somewhere in the distance.

Polly tells me, "They stay coupled for half an hour after they have sex."

I'm still inside her, softer than I was a few minutes ago, our bodies dappled in the moonlight coming through the cabin window.

Outside, a flowering dogwood stirs in the wind. The branches scratch against our window like the nails of a wild animal, and I think about the wolves: running, baying, in heat.

Coupled.

We can hear a choir singing something about Jesus when we awaken. It's late Sunday afternoon.

There's a small Baptist church with peeling white paint down the dirt road from our cabin. Polly and I stand in a grove of black walnut trees, listening to the voices rise and fall in the humid air.

A bell above the screen door rings when I go into the office. There's a sign on the wood paneling behind the main desk:

WELCOME TO THE TRAIL OF TEARS AUTO COURT. IN GOD WE TRUST; ALL OTHERS PAY CASH.

It's probably not a bad idea.

On the way here we drove by a shack constructed out of Kotex cartons. Some dirty-looking kids pointed at us as we passed. I don't think they'd ever seen a white convertible.

The old guy who owns the auto court says, "That's a nice-lookin' car you got."

I can hear a radio playing in the back room. Someone's singing "What Do I Have to Do to Get It?"

"Thanks, I gave it to my girlfriend for her birthday."

"Nobody ever give me nothin'," he says. He doesn't have any front teeth, and he whistles when he talks. "Nothin' but grief, that is. The dust storms blowed everything away, then the bank come round. I wuz in Oklahoma at the time. I told 'em I wuz gonna fight if they come to take my farm. Well, sir, I didn't put up much of a battle, but I set fire to my crops, burnt my house and p'izened my cattle. I guess I showed the bastids."

"I guess you did," I say.

I give the old guy a ten-dollar bill and tell him to keep the change, then he and I go out onto the porch together.

"Did you hear about the shootin' over near Branson?" he asks.

I nod, no, listening to the choir. Now they're singing "Shall We Gather at the River?" but it's not a question.

There's an authority to their voices.

I wish I were that sure of something.

"Must have been a hundred cops an' G-men come down on this auto court near there, and they come in shootin'," the old guy says. "Wuzn't a window that wuzn't broke in the whole place and three dogs and a couple of cats wuz shot to death."

"What happened?"

"I guess they thought Pretty Boy Floyd and Dillinger wuz meetin' there, plannin' a job, recoverin' from their wounds." He cackles. "Who the hell knows?

"When they rushed into the place they didn't find nothin' but a bunch of people in their Sunday best cowerin' behind a sofa and an old darkie with a broom. Them agents called it a deadly weapon and took it away, but the announcer didn't say what happened to the darkie."

The old guy cackles again.

"If they ever wuz there, Dillinger and Floyd got away."

"I'm glad to hear it," I say.

The Wolf River Cemetery was across the road from a rural church with peeling white paint in Pall Mall, Tennessee.

Billie and I watched the parishioners come out of the church, sweating, then cross the small highway to the cemetery in their Sunday suits and dresses. Most of them carried flowers to put next to the graves.

It was Memorial Day weekend, and I wondered why the paint on country churches always seemed to be peeling. Probably because the parishioners were poor.

A man in a faded blue suit said, "There's Sergeant York." He was tall and gaunt and he bent over a grave, lowering himself slowly until he rested on one knee, setting a single red rose on a grave.

It was hard to imagine Sergeant York killing Germans—or anyone—but he'd been the most decorated soldier in the Great War.

The man who'd identified the sergeant pointed to the farmhouse across the field next to the cemetery and said, "Alvin lives over yonder," and there was something reverential in his voice. The woman nodded as Sergeant York stood.

He was wearing a baggy gray pinstripe suit, and he held his hat in both hands. It had begun to drizzle, and shadows were pale, fragile things that followed you across the cemetery like apparitions in the bleak light. There were a lot of ferns in the valley.

A large marble angel hovered over one of the graves, but Billie and I didn't stop to look at it because of the rain. It was coming down harder as we crossed the small highway to our car.

We watched the rain come down on the angel and the small church and on Sergeant York as he left the cemetery, slowly, his suit baggy, his face glowing.

The rain came down from the Smoky Mountains, swirling, but it was easy to imagine it was raining everywhere: Coming down in torrents on the living and the dead.

GEORGE NELSON

"I don't get it," I say. "I'm the guy who planned this job, but I'm supposed to watch the car while you two go into the bank?"

"Yeah," Homer says.

He picks at a piece of gristle caught between his teeth.

We all ordered the special, pork chop sandwiches, because the twat waiting on us recommended it.

The food may be lousy, but we can see Merchants National from our table. The assistant postmaster ought to be making his weekly deposit in a few minutes.

The thermometer above the bank says it's ninety-four degrees.

It must be the hottest day of the year in South Bend, and I'm the guy who gets to stand in the street.

"What kind of a deal is that?" I ask.

"It's the luck of the draw," Homer says.

"There wasn't any fuckin' draw," I say.

Homer snaps his toothpick, dropping it into an ashtray.

"Why don't you quit sniveling?"

"You shouldn't talk to me like that. Tell him, John. It ain't nice."

"What do you have to worry about? Newspapers aren't saying you're dead because you haven't robbed a bank recently. Why don't the two of you shut up and eat your damn sandwiches?"

It's almost twelve when I park the Hudson in front of the bank.

I lean against the car, one hand in the open window on the driver's side, clutching the machine gun, while Homer and John cross the sidewalk. They're wearing overalls and straw hats.

They could be the fuckin' Bobbsey Twins.

The car vibrates because I kept the engine running.

I never did like Hudsons.

Across the street, there's a huge banner hanging down from the marquee of the State Theater. AIR COOLED. *Stolen Sweets* is playing.

Homer and John go into the bank.

Stolen Sweets. I like that.

Some kid walks by, gawking.

"What're you lookin' at?"

"Nothing."

"Then get the hell out of here. Aren't you supposed to be in school or something?"

"Nah, there ain't any school on Saturday. Anybody knows that."

The kid can't be more than twelve.

"You'd better scram if you don't want to get hurt."

"Who's going to hurt me?" he asks, then someone fires a pistol inside the bank.

The kid starts running, and a fat cop who's directing traffic on the corner blows his whistle as I grab the machine gun.

209

Some fool comes out of the jewelry store across the street, holding a pistol, aiming at me, firing. I can feel the slug thud against my bulletproof vest before I hear the shot, before I squeeze the trigger on the Thompson, staggering backwards. I shoot high, knocking out the windows in the jewelry store and the windshield of a car, the cop running, blowing his whistle. When I hit him with a burst from the Thompson, he's flung backwards, as if he's learned the secret of flight, then his body hits the pavement like a bag of wet laundry.

At least he stopped blowing the goddamn whistle.

I watch John and Homer coming out of the bank, then someone jumps me from behind, putting an arm around my throat. "I've got you," he says, but I twist my body, throwing him. When he hits the window of a bookstore, he shatters the glass, falling backwards, his arms flailing. He can't be more than sixteen, and he has a surprised bloody look, a shard, like a glass arrow, stuck in his throat, blood spurting onto his white shirt. He leans against a table filled with best-sellers, trying to hold himself up with his bloody hands, staring at the books as if he's never seen one before, his eyes glazed, disbelieving, then he slumps from my sight.

What's wrong with kids these days?

A bullet grazes Homer's head, and he stumbles, touching his forehead with his right hand. His straw hat falls off, and there's blood where part of his scalp used to be. "Come on, come on," I say, firing the Thompson, "this ain't the time to pray." Homer's on his knees, but John helps him up, slowly . . . slowly. They almost fall into the car.

"Did you get the money?" I ask.

John's clutching the canvas bag they took into the bank, but I can't tell if it's full or not.

"You sonofabitch," John says, "I thought this was supposed to be 'easy as pie,' but you had to kill that cop."

"Yeah, wasn't it a beautiful sight?"

The sky's a pale-bluish purple when we abandon the Hudson at the edge of a small town near the Illinois border.

A transient worker sits like a hunchback on a box that says FANDANGO HOT SAUCE. He looks into a mirror he's attached to the door on the driver's side of a broken-down truck with Texas license plates, shaving with a straight razor. He probably works in the fields all day, picking cucumbers, and he'd slit his throat if he didn't have three crying kids and a frail wife.

Sometimes I think I have it bad.

Homer says, "I seem to be all right," touching his scalp.

"Why shouldn't you be? The bullet just grazed you."

"What do you mean, it just grazed me? It tore half my fuckin' head off."

"At least you don't have to worry about your brains leakin' out."

"What that's supposed to mean?"

"You figure it out," I say.

When we come into the town, two colored women are sitting on a wooden bench beneath a sign that says DOUBLE-DIP CONES, 5 CENTS, and there's a Popsicle sign on the grocery screen door.

They're wearing floral dresses and straw hats, but they probably live in the shantytown next to the town dump where the smell of decaying things hangs in the putrid air and they don't have a nickel between them. The fumes from the rotting meat and vegetables obscure the moon.

I give one of them a dollar and John asks, "You ladies wouldn't happen to know where we can buy a car, would you?"

but they just look at him, the whites of their eyes rolling like tumblers on a slot machine, their lips blubbery.

We buy a Chrysler sedan for a thousand bucks, then we divide thirty-thousand dollars in a small grove of trees at the far end of town.

Some children are swimming, naked, in the nearby river. You need a flyswatter to beat away the mosquitoes, but it's a better place than the one where I grew up. There aren't any nuns beating the kids with rulers.

Homer counts the bills out, placing them in three piles.

"Careful," I say, "don't bleed on the goddamn money."

JOHN DILLINGER

Homer's dividing the money when I see her walking along the river where the children are swimming.

She's wearing a white dress and gloves, and the sunlight filters through the parasol she's holding. Her wrists are fragile and her face is a blur in the soft light, as if someone had photographed her and left the portrait in the sun too long so that it faded.

There's something ethereal about her as she walks along the river in the quivering light that comes through the trees, through the parasol. She almost seems to glide along the riverbank, and I run after her.

Baby Face yells, "Where're you goin'?" but I don't answer.

I've seen her before, not just in Wahoo or Mooresville.

She was wearing a white dress, and I think she was sleeping, I remember I cried, watching her, but I don't know why. I must have been three.

I'm out of breath when I reach the river. I can hear the sound of my heart coming up into my ears and the screams of the children and the splashing water, but she's gone. It's as if she evaporated into a beam of light, and there aren't any footprints in the wet sand.

_____ HOMER VAN METER

John's pale, out of breath, when he comes back from the river, and his hands are shaking. He looks like someone who's had a heart attack.

"What was that all about?" I ask.

"I don't know," he says.

_____ JOHN DILLINGER

"You're going to get yourself killed, living with that gang," Homer says.

"I'm not going to live with a gang. I'm going to live with Polly. The only other people in the building are Anna and her son, and they're harmless."

"John, no one's harmless when there's a fifteen-thousand-dollar reward out for you, dead or alive."

"We all have to die sometime."

"Yeah," Homer says, "but why rush things?"

Some kids are setting off firecrackers on the sidewalk in front of Polly's apartment. They watch me carrying trunks filled with machine guns, pistols, bulletproof vests, and ammunition up the steps.

Tonight there'll be fireworks over Lake Michigan. Polly and I can watch them from the rooftop.

One of the kids yells, "Hey, mister, whatever you got in them trunks must weigh a ton. What you got in there?"

"Machine guns."

"Yeah, sure, tell me another one," the kid says.

"I don't know if there's enough space for the two of us and all your guns," Polly says.

"Sure there is. All you have to do is get rid of some of your shoes. You must have thirty pair in the closet."

"You certainly don't know much about women," Polly says.

Some kids are running through the water coming from an open hydrant on the corner. Polly and I watch them from our kitchen window, drinking lemonade and sweating.

Polly says, "I used to like summer, but you could feel the air move in the country. I grew up on a farm, and we had a little pond on the place and lots of chickens. My brother and I liked to play barefooted in the bin where the cracked corn was stored.

"One day my father brought home a baby goat and he let us play with it in the bin, but the goat ate so much corn that it puffed up and died."

Polly's wearing a low-cut dress. I can see the beads of perspiration on her breasts.

"Summertime was when my father brought in loose hay to store in a shed that was attached to the two-story barn. After the hay was stacked in the shed, we liked to get on the second floor and jump into the haystack."

The kids run through the water from the hydrant, pointing their fingers at each other and shouting, "Bang, bang."

Some of them fall down, pretending they're shot.

I remember playing cowboys and Indians in the barn behind Dad's house. I always wanted to be Jesse James because I hated being nobody and poor.

Polly says, "We had a horse and a cow, but not quite enough room to pasture them on our own farm. We used the neighbor's pasture and every evening after milking, we'd take a bucket of milk to the neighbors in exchange for the use of the pasture.

"I remember one time when I was about nine—my brother would have been about four—we decided we'd get on the horse bareback and hold onto the mane. We mounted the horse, Harold held onto me, and the first thing I knew the horse was galloping toward this big tree.

"I saw a branch protruding and ducked but Harold didn't know what was coming and the branch hit him and he was knocked off the horse. When I went over to him, he was crying, but I could tell he wasn't hurt.

"Dad gave me a spanking I never forgot when he found out about it. I didn't think it was fair."

"Most things aren't," I say.

We watch the fireworks explode over the lake.

Polly says, "I hemorrhaged one Fourth of July. My husband and I had come home from a dance, and I was swallowing blood. I spit a mouthful of it into the sink, turning the tile red, but there was more blood welling up in my throat. I'd had my tonsils out, and I'd felt something . . . ripping in my throat since then. My husband put towels underneath me so I wouldn't get blood on our couch. That night I knew he was a fool, that I was going to divorce him."

"My wife divorced me when I was in prison," I say. "I'd looked forward to going back home sometime, and suddenly there wasn't any home to go back to. I began to know how you feel when your heart's breaking."

I watch the sky turn red and green and blue. It's as if someone pinned a butterfly against the night, its flailing wings pushing back the darkness.

"I didn't know you were married."

"It's something I don't like to talk about," I say.

I put my head between her legs, seeking her center. I can hear the wind coming off the lake. Her warm thighs press against my cheeks.

The crescent moon glides across the dark. I dream: I'm a little boy in Indiana. I'm running through a field of violets and peonies, catching butterflies and eating them. As fast as I catch them, I put them into my mouth, savoring their flavor. It's a warm day. I'm sweating. There are so many beautiful colors. I want to taste them all.

Polly watches me get into the tub, smiling, and I tell her, "It not only floats, it walks across the water."

She lowers herself onto me as I lean back in the tub, watching my penis disappear. Polly's red hair gleams in the morning light.

The water splashes and the warm sun comes through the little window next to the sink.

We smile at one another when I come.

"That was the cleanest sex I ever had," I say.

HOMER VAN METER

"I tell you, John, we'd make a fortune. We dictate the story of our lives, then we hire this guy to prepare the material for publication."

"What guy?"

"I don't know. Maybe the guy who wrote *Little Caesar.* Someone who has a feel for the kind of lives we've led."

"How does he know what kind of lives we've led?"

"Don't be so goddamn practical," I say. "We tell him the stuff he needs to know, and he makes up the rest. Then we hire someone else to make a movie about us, one of those things that tell people crime doesn't pay."

"Why would we want to do that?"

"'Cause it's what they want to hear. It's got a message for the little guy. See? We'd exhibit our machine guns, our pistols, our bulletproof vests, everything. Then we'd give the youth of

America a warning: We'd tell them not to follow in our footsteps, tell them how we're hunted like rats—"

John laughs. "Like rats, huh?"

"Yeah. Hunted like rats and driven from one crime to another to raise the money we need to buy another day's protection. Isn't it great?"

"It sounds pretty horrible to me."

"That's the idea. Everyone would want to hear that crap. We'd probably make a million bucks."

"I think we'd better stick with the banks," John says.

JOHN DILLINGER

Polly. . . .

You're leaning over me, smiling, when I awaken.

Your eyelids glitter because you didn't wash off your makeup from last night.

As you move your lips along my body, drops of blue and silver and pink glitter fall from your eyelids, landing on my chest and penis like a fine rain; and the feel of you is fine, too.

I reach up touching your breasts as I slide into you.

Your pubic hair sparkles—blue and silver and pink—as we move together, our bodies moist in the early-morning heat.

The whole world glitters.

MELVIN PURVIS

The woman sits on a straight-backed wooden chair, her hands folded on her lap. She's wearing a tweed skirt and white blouse and she could be in a church, but she used to run a whorehouse and she's come to make a deal.

"What do you have to tell us, Anna?"

Clegg's standing next to the window.

I remember the time he questioned someone he thought would lead us to Dillinger. Clegg held the guy out the window by his ankles, then dropped him nineteen stories and said, "Oops."

The guy landed on his head, and it took the sanitation workers an hour to scrape him off the pavement.

Half my life has been spent dealing with whores and gangsters, and I've spent the other half looking for them. Sometimes I think my mother was right; I should have joined the navy.

"I give you John Dillinger for promise not to deport me," Anna says.

She's been in this country fifteen years, and she still doesn't know how to speak English.

"Keep talking," Clegg says.

"I don't care about no reward. FBI can keep money as long as I don't be sent back to Romania."

If they don't deport her for running a whorehouse, they ought to deport her for her bad grammar.

"I think we can help you, Anna."

I can feel her tension when I touch her shoulder.

"Dillinger, his girlfriend and me be coming out of movie house next Sunday night. We be going to the Biograph or Marbro. If we go to Biograph I wear orange skirt. If we go to Marbro I wear blue skirt. You watch us when we come out of apartment."

I say, "That'll be fine, Anna. We appreciate your help."

When she leaves the office Clegg asks, "Do you really think the Immigration Department will go along with a deal not to deport her?"

"Who cares," I ask, "as long as we get Dillinger?"

I tell Polly, "We should have gone to the beach," but we watch a baseball game in Jackson Park because Anna's son is on one of the teams.

Seventeen people died from heat prostration yesterday, and more are supposed to die today.

Why would anyone play baseball in this weather?

Why would anyone attend a game, sitting in the bleachers?

I can barely breathe.

There's no shade, and the temperature's 103 degrees and rising. Most people don't have jobs to go to today, but they're dying at the beach, suffocating in tiny apartments across the city, dying in church.

"I never liked Sundays," Polly says.

People are even dying in the movies.

Polly, Anna, and I go to see *Manhattan Melodrama* in the evening.

William Powell plays a prosecuting attorney who convicts his pal, Clark Gable, of murder. Gable's offered life imprisonment, but he tells Powell he'd rather get the electric chair.

I don't blame him.

MELVIN PURVIS

I've got twenty men, heavily armed, waiting in alleys and around corners, standing in front of barbershops and bookie joints, waiting outside the Biograph in the darkness.

I'll give them the signal when I see Dillinger: I'm supposed to strike a match, lighting a cigar. Then I'll exhale, blowing the match out.

It's 10:35, and the temperature's still over a hundred when the Sage woman, Polly, and Dillinger come out of the Biograph.

Anna's wearing a skirt that looks red in the blinking light. She drops back a couple of steps as the three of them leave the theater.

I light my cigar.

Polly's hanging onto Dillinger's arm, laughing, when she turns to look at Anna, but one of my men shoves Polly aside, pushing her into the gutter, and the others open fire before Dillinger can turn around. He lurches forward, as if he's going to make a run for it, his body propelled by the bullets. He staggers a step or two, then he falls face-forward onto the bricks leading to an alley beside the Biograph.

Polly's crying, "You murdered him," leaning over his body, but my men pull her away when I run up to him. She stands there screaming, "Murderers!"

When I examine the body, I can see one bullet entered the back of Dillinger's neck coming out his right cheek, and there's a bloody spot on his left side. Blood's pumping out of three other wounds, leaking onto the bricks. Dillinger's still alive five minutes later when an ambulance arrives, but he dies on the way to the Alexian Brothers Hospital and his body's taken to the Cook County Morgue. Some people take a long time dying.

I slap Polly across the face, hard, rocking her. She has one foot in the gutter and the other one on the curb, and she looks like she's going to puke. The bitch has always had one foot in the gutter. That's what attracted her to Dillinger.

"Why don't you shut up?" I say.

Mr. Hoover's going to give me a promotion.

JOHN HERBERT DILLINGER

Johnnie's laid out in a lavender coffin at the McCready Funeral Home on Sheridan Road. Thousands of people gather outside, waiting to see the body.

I leave the funeral home with the Rev. Fillmore, who married me and Johnnie's mother and who was my pastor at the Hillside Christian Church. I say, "My boy, my boy."

I tell the reporters, "They didn't give Johnnie a chance. They shot him down from behind in cold blood. I wouldn't want to see a dog shot down like that. Why, he had fifteen or twenty men trying to kill him. That isn't fair. It was an execution. No attempt worthy of the name was made to capture him alive."

Then the Rev. Fillmore and I walk down the steps to the car that's waiting to take me home.

POLLY HAMILTON

The Rev. Fillmore ends his sermon by saying, "We should eliminate the forces that cause men to become gangsters through educational processes, not violence. Given the proper encouragement, who knows what John might have accomplished?"

Then a quartet sings, "God Will Take Care of You," and a second hymn, "We Say Good Night Down Here and Good Morning Up There."

There's a tent over the grave because of the threatening weather, and it begins to rain moments before John's body is lowered into the earth.

The rain won't wash away my tears.

When I'm leaving the cemetery reporters ask me for a statement and I tell them, "I was crazy about Johnnie. He had a marvelous personality, and he was kind and good to me. He was interested in everything that was going on, and I don't just mean cops and robbers, but daily events.

"He was crazy about movies, and we went to nightclubs. I always got a thrill out of going around in cabs with him. We cabbed everywhere.

"He was broad-shouldered and had a fascinating smile, especially when he was playing cards. He loved to play pinochle and rummy. Penny-ante stuff, a nickel limit, so no one would lose much.

"Twice he gave me money so a friend and I could go to the World's Fair, and when I told him I couldn't go to the beach because I didn't have a decent bathing suit he handed me forty dollars and said I should buy one.

"We had a lot of fun. It's surprising how much fun we had."